PUFFIN BOOKS

Winston
and
the
Marmalade
Cat

Praise for Megan Rix

'If you love Michael Morpurgo, you'll
enjoy this' *Sunday Express*

'A moving tale told with warmth, kindliness and
lashings of good sense that lovers of Dick King-Smith
will especially appreciate' *The Times*

'Every now and then a writer comes along with a unique
way of storytelling. Meet Megan Rix . . . her novels are
deeply moving and will strike a chord with animal lovers'
LoveReading

'A perfect story for animal lovers and lovers of adventure
stories' *Travelling Book Company*

Praise from Megan's young readers

'I never liked reading until one day I was in
Waterstones and I picked up some books. One was . . .
called *The Bomber Dog*. I loved it so much I couldn't
put it down' Luke, 8

'I found this book amazing' Nayah, 11

'EPIC BOOK!!!' Jessica, 13

MEGAN RIX is the recent winner of the Stockton and Shrewsbury Children's Book Awards, and has been shortlisted for numerous other children's book awards. She lives with her husband by a river in England. When she's not writing, she can be found walking her gorgeous dogs, Bella and Freya, who are often in the river.

Books by Megan Rix

THE BOMBER DOG

ECHO COME HOME

THE GREAT ESCAPE

THE GREAT FIRE DOGS

THE HERO PUP

THE RUNAWAYS

A SOLDIER'S FRIEND

THE VICTORY DOGS

www.meganrix.com

'One of my favourite books' Chloe, Year 8

Winston
and
the
Marmalade
Cat

megan rix

PUFFIN

PUFFIN BOOKS

UK | USA | Canada | Ireland | Australia
India | New Zealand | South Africa

Puffin Books is part of the Penguin Random House group of companies
whose addresses can be found at global.penguinrandomhouse.com.

www.penguin.co.uk
www.puffin.co.uk
www.ladybird.co.uk

Penguin
Random House
UK

First published 2017

001

Text copyright © Megan Rix, 2017
Cover illustration by Angelo Rinaldi

The moral right of the author has been asserted

Set in 13/20 pt Baskerville MT
Typeset by Jouve (UK), Milton Keynes
Printed in Great Britain by Clays Ltd, St Ives plc

A CIP catalogue record for this book is available from the British Library

ISBN: 978–0–141–38569–3

All correspondence to:
Puffin Books
Penguin Random House Children's
80 Strand, London WC2R 0RL

For animal lovers and their furry friends

Chapter 1

The small kitten raced across the icy wasteland after his prey, but the yellow autumn leaf was held by the wind and flew just ahead of him, out of reach of the kitten's paws.

Determined not to lose it, the kitten ran on, leaving the den where his mother and his brothers and sisters still slept far behind.

When the wind finally released the leaf and it dropped to the ground, the kitten pounced on it with a crunch and stared down at his prey, triumphant. Then he spotted another leaf dancing in the wind, another leaf that needed to be caught before it could escape. He released the first one to dash after the second, but then another leaf fell to the side of him and he darted after that instead.

Sometimes he jumped up to catch the fleeing leaves mid-air. Sometimes he pounced on them when they hit the ground, but there were too many crisp late November leaves for one small kitten to be able to catch them all.

The kitten looked back again at the hawthorn bush that his family was hidden in and gave a miaow, but none of them came to help.

He watched as a sparrow flew above him, then spied a worm that disappeared back below the ground before the hungry kitten could reach it.

In front of him, the kitten spied a long, thin metal tunnel lying on the ground. When he poked his head inside it he saw a mouse on the grass at the other end. The kitten's heart beat fast with excitement and he crouched low as he squeezed into the tunnel and headed towards it.

A moment later the kitten gave a cry as the tunnel lifted off the ground. He slid forward and was covered with thick, black wet mud that stung his eyes. He tried to cry out again but the mud went into his mouth and made him cough.

Worst of all came a great clang followed by a terrifying roar.

The kitten trembled as the roar turned into a juddering hum, and he curled up into a muddy ball in the darkness.

Alone and very afraid.

Chapter 2

'Morning, Callie,' nine-year-old Harry said, as he released the bolt on her RSPCA cage.

The yellow Labrador looked up at him with her big brown eyes and wagged her tail.

'Don't be too long now,' said Mr Jenner, who ran the centre, as Harry clipped on Callie's lead. 'I don't want you being late for school again.'

'We'll be quick,' Harry promised as he stroked Callie's soft furry head.

The Labrador looked up at Harry every now and again as they headed out of the centre and down the street.

'I like taking you for walks most of all,' Harry told Callie as she trotted along beside him. 'Because you don't pull on your lead.'

Some of the other dogs got so excited and pulled so much that Harry felt like his arms were going to fall off when he took them out for a walk. Not that he blamed them. Going for a walk was very exciting when you were stuck in a cage all day.

'I wish you could be my dog,' Harry said, when they reached the corner and had to turn back.

He wished he could have a dog, a cat or even a hamster or a budgie of his own, but he knew his parents wouldn't let him. At least he got to spend time with lots of animals at the RSPCA.

*

At school they were learning about the Second World War, which had ended seventeen years ago in 1945. Harry's teacher Mrs Dunbar was telling them all about Winston Churchill who was Prime Minister during the war and led the country to victory.

'We owe a great deal to him,' she told the class. 'And we should feel honoured that he's chosen to make his main home here in this part of Kent, not far from our school.'

Harry scowled. The war hadn't done his family any good and he didn't care where Winston Churchill lived. He drew a picture of Callie on the back of his exercise book instead.

William, who sat next to Harry, drew a picture of Winston Churchill's hand in the famous victory salute and then added a big smile to it.

Harry sighed and shook his head at his friend. He glanced up at the clock on the wall.

Only ten minutes left before school was over and he could head back to help at the RSPCA centre.

As soon as the bell rang Harry and William pulled on their coats and ran over to the bike rack.

'That bike's too big for you, Harry,' William said, as Harry pulled out the heavy black-framed 1940s roadster with a basket on the front.

William had a brand-new 1962 three-speed Raleigh bike. He'd got it for his birthday a few weeks ago and never stopped talking about it.

Harry just shrugged. He didn't care that his bike was too big and more than twenty years old. It was a bike and Harry hadn't had a bike until Mr Jenner said he could borrow this one: 'Provided you don't mind running an errand on it for me from time to time.'

Mr Jenner knew just about everything there was to know about animals and Harry wanted to be just like him one day.

Because the bike was a bit too big for him, Harry wasn't able sit on the saddle and have his feet flat on the ground at the same time. He pushed down on the right pedal while he was standing up and then hopped on quickly and pushed down on the left pedal. It was a bit tricky and wobbly, but he managed.

'See you tomorrow,' Harry called out to William, as he rode off.

He wasn't far from the RSPCA centre, cycling down Tindale Street, when one of the school dinner ladies, Mrs Yarrow, pulled a handkerchief from the pocket of her long apron and waved it at him.

'Harry! Harry – stop!' she called to him, as she hurried out of her front garden gate in her slippers.

It wasn't easy to stop the bicycle once he'd started pedalling it. Not without falling off. But Harry just managed to get his foot on the ground before the bicycle toppled over.

'Yes, Mrs Yarrow?' he said.

'There's an animal trapped in there,' Mrs Yarrow said, pointing at an old rusty pipe sticking out of her lavender bush. 'I think it's a cat. I heard it scratching and mewling, but it didn't sound very strong, poor thing. I had a look but I couldn't see anything and my arms are too big to get down the pipe, but maybe you can? The pipe fell off one of those scrap-metal lorries. They really should take more care on these winding country roads.'

Harry had been helping at his local RSPCA centre for two whole months, but this was the first time he'd actually been asked to rescue an animal himself and he wanted to do it properly.

He tried to remember what Mr Jenner had told him about rescuing cats. There was something important. He could picture Mr Jenner in his head, looking at him over his half-moon spectacles and giving him advice.

Oh yes, that was it!

The most important thing is never to try to capture a stray or feral cat with your bare hands. A lost cat will probably be scared and you can't predict how it will react.

'Cat scratches and bites can be very dangerous and cause infections,' Mr Jenner had added. But Harry didn't have any special protective gloves with him and this was an emergency. The cat, if it was a cat, needed his help and it needed his help right now.

'It's pretty mucky and very smelly inside the pipe,' Mrs Yarrow told Harry as he took off his coat and rolled up his jumper sleeves. 'I don't even like to think what it was used for before it ended up on that lorry.'

Harry pushed his hand inside the pipe but couldn't feel anything except sticky, oozy muck. Maybe the cat had got itself out of it somehow already. Harry felt around in the mud some more, hoping the poor creature was OK and didn't decide to bite him.

Harry wondered where the cat had come from and whether it was a stray or if someone, somewhere, was looking for it. According to Mr Jenner there was a big difference between stray and feral cats. A stray cat was one that had been living with people but then got lost or been abandoned. A feral cat was a wild cat that wasn't used to people at all. A stray might let you touch it, but a feral cat would probably bite and scratch you.

There! He could feel something and it wasn't mud. Definitely not mud. Harry pulled at it and a moment later he found himself holding a kitten that was covered from head to tail in slimy, stinking, thick black mud. Harry couldn't even see a spot of its fur under all the mess. The kitten gave a little cry as it opened its bright blue eyes and stared at its rescuer.

'Oh, the poor mite,' Mrs Yarrow said.

Harry cradled the muddy kitten to him. He could feel its little heart beating very fast as it started to make tiny whimpering sounds. Harry knew he needed to get the kitten to Mr Jenner at the RSPCA as soon as possible.

'Thanks, Mrs Yarrow,' he said, as he wrapped the kitten inside his coat so that only its head was poking out. He put the kitten and coat into the bicycle basket, pushed down on the pedal with his foot and sped off towards the RSPCA centre.

Mr Jenner would know what to do for the best.

Chapter 3

'Mr Jenner,' Harry shouted as he cycled into the yard, ringing the bicycle bell, and almost colliding with a shiny black Rolls-Royce that was parked in the driveway. 'Mr Jenner!'

Harry pressed on the old bicycle's brakes at the same time as he put his foot on the ground and came to a squealing, wobbly stop.

Mr Jenner walked out of the centre with a distinguished-looking man in a dark suit. A uniformed chauffeur, waiting inside the

Rolls-Royce, immediately jumped out and stood next to the passenger door of the car.

Harry liked cars very much and usually he'd have wanted to take a closer look at it, but today there were more important things to worry about. He wished Mr Jenner would stop talking.

'We've got lots of dogs looking for new homes,' Mr Jenner was saying. 'I'm sure Sir Winston would love a dog. Perhaps even a British bull-dog? Or Callie, she's a yellow Labrador with the sweetest nature, and smart too.'

But the man in the suit shook his head.

'Sir Winston does love dogs, very much, but his miniature poodle Rufus died earlier this year and he was very attached to him. He can't bear to have another.'

'What about a bird then?' Mr Jenner asked. 'People don't often think of birds needing rehoming, but they do.'

While Mr Jenner was speaking Harry tried to get his attention without speaking himself. He pointed at the bicycle basket urgently, but although Mr Jenner glanced over at him he didn't stop his conversation, much to Harry's frustration. It was cold without his coat on and Harry rubbed his hands up and down his arms and stomped his feet to keep himself warm.

'Unfortunately, Sir Winston lost his budgerigar Toby this year too, when he was in Monte Carlo. No one was able to find him. I think this time it has to be a cat, preferably a marmalade cat,' the man said.

Harry looked down worriedly at the tiny kitten whose big blue eyes stared back at him. He wondered whether he should lift the kitten out of the bicycle basket and carry it over to Mr Jenner. Why was he taking so long?

'Well, I'm sorry we don't have any marmalade cats here at the moment, Mr Colville,' Mr Jenner said. 'But if we do get one, or I hear of any, I'll let you know immediately.'

'It really is most urgent,' the man said. 'Sir Winston's birthday is in two days' time. He used to have a favourite marmalade cat called Tango many years ago. There's a painting of him with Sir Winston and his wife at Chartwell. I just know he'd love another marmalade cat.'

'I'll do my very best, Mr Colville,' Mr Jenner promised, as the chauffeur opened the passenger door and the man got in. 'Have you tried the other RSPCAs and cat rehoming centres?'

'Yes, and they've all promised to keep a look out.'

'I'm sure you'll find one before Sir Winston's birthday,' Mr Jenner said.

'I hope so,' said Mr Colville as he got in the car and the chauffeur closed the door.

'Mr Jenner!' Harry hissed, but Mr Jenner waved his hand at him to shush until the Rolls-Royce had driven out of the yard.

Chapter 4

'Mr Jenner!' Harry shouted, quickly pushing his bike over to him as soon as the car had gone.

'What is it, Harry?' Mr Jenner asked him.

'A kitten,' Harry said. 'I rescued a kitten.'

Harry pointed to his coat in the bicycle basket where the kitten lay, unmoving.

Mr Jenner carefully lifted the tiny creature from Harry's coat.

'It is . . . it is going to be OK, isn't it?' Harry said. The kitten was so small and fragile. It looked helpless in Mr Jenner's big hands and so covered in mud that none of its fur could even be seen.

Mr Jenner checked the kitten's nose and mouth and then he headed back into the centre with Harry following closely at his heels.

'His fur will need a good clean, but his airways look clear, thank goodness. Although I'm sure he must have swallowed some mud because his mouth is muddy. Let's try him with a little kitten formula,' Mr Jenner said. 'He doesn't look old enough to have been separated from his mother yet.'

'He fell off the back of a lorry,' Harry said. 'Stuck in a pipe. But I don't know where he came from.'

'He's very thin,' Mr Jenner said. 'But not starving. Most likely a feral kitten that's got lost. Ones as young as this can make good pets. If he were older it'd be harder to tame him. Adult feral cats take a great deal of time and patience because they're not used to people and shy away from them.'

Mr Jenner gave Harry the kitten to hold while he mixed some goat's milk with an egg yolk and a little sugar in a small bowl. Harry saw that some of the mud from the kitten had got on to Mr Jenner's RSPCA uniform, but he knew he wouldn't care about that.

'Let's see if he'll eat this,' Mr Jenner said.

He put the bowl on the ground and Harry knelt down and set the kitten on the floor. He didn't even know if the tiny thing would be strong enough to stand. But it could, staggering and trembling a little as if it was very weak and tired.

'Give him a little on your finger. If he's a wild, feral kitten, which I think he must be, he won't be used to a bowl,' Mr Jenner said.

Harry dipped his finger in the formula and the kitten hungrily licked the mixture from it. Harry did it again and then again.

The little kitten watched Harry's finger going into the bowl and then he put his furry head into the bowl too.

Harry smiled as he watched the kitten lapping at the mixture.

'I know you said not to try to rescue a cat with my bare hands,' Harry said to Mr Jenner. 'But I really didn't have a choice.'

'You did the right thing, Harry,' Mr Jenner said, clapping him on the shoulder. 'This little chap owes his life to you.'

The kitten stopped lapping the formula, looked up at Harry and mewed as if he were agreeing.

Once the kitten's tummy was full and it had been on the litter tray, Mr Jenner said it was time for the kitten to have a bath.

'It'll be even harder to get that thick mud off him once it's fully dried on.'

He filled a large tin bowl with warm water and set it on the floor next to Harry and the kitten.

'You can bathe him, Harry,' Mr Jenner said. 'He already trusts you. Put him in the bowl. Careful now.'

Harry was worried the kitten would be frightened by the water, but he didn't struggle at all. Harry didn't know if it was because the kitten was so weak and exhausted or if the kitten trusted him not to hurt him.

'I thought cats weren't supposed to like water,' Harry laughed as the kitten started to purr.

'Some cats and kittens do like water,' Mr Jenner said. 'Some of them even swim.'

Harry had never heard of cats doing that before, although he knew that big cats, like tigers, could.

'I bet this one will be a swimmer,' he said. Or at least he hoped so.

As more mud came off the kitten Harry was very surprised to find it wasn't black, or charcoal grey or even tabby-coated. Underneath all that dirt was a kitten with a beautiful marmalade coat.

Chapter 5

Mr Jenner chuckled. 'Bit of a coincidence a
marmalade kitten turning up now. Although I
think Mr Colville might be after an older cat
for Sir Winston.'

Once all the mud was washed away they
could see that the kitten had a white bib and
four white paws as well.

'You smell a lot better now too,' Harry told
the kitten, as Mr Jenner handed him a soft
towel. Before long the kitten was helping to dry

himself by licking at his fur while Harry gently blotted him with the towel.

Harry smiled as the kitten stopped licking himself and licked Harry's hand with his tiny raspy tongue instead.

The words slipped out before Harry could stop them.

'Could I adopt him?'

He knew that sometimes the people who rescued animals for the RSPCA were the ones that got to keep them.

'Oh,' Mr Jenner said, surprised. 'Well, I don't see why not, if you're sure. Feral kittens don't belong to anyone and you are the one who found him. Without you, well, I don't like to think what might have happened to him.'

'I'd look after him really well,' Harry said. And love him lots, he told himself.

'I know you would,' Mr Jenner said. 'But you'd have to have permission from your mum and dad first. And they should meet him before you take him home and there should really be a home check too.'

The more Mr Jenner spoke the more a tiny voice inside Harry's head said that maybe he wouldn't be allowed to keep the kitten. But he wanted to take him home so badly that he ignored it.

'I'll let you know first thing tomorrow morning,' he said.

The little kitten was more than half asleep as he gave him back to Mr Jenner.

'See you in the morning, kitty,' he said. 'I'll be here early.'

'See you tomorrow, Harry,' Mr Jenner called after him as Harry pulled on his muddy coat, ran out of the centre, jumped on his bike and raced home as fast as the creaky old thing would go.

Chapter 6

Harry's mother was still at the hospital where she worked as a nurse, but his father was home, as usual. He didn't work any more and he was sitting in the same armchair he always sat in.

'Dad, Dad!' Harry cried excitedly, as he ran into the room. 'Guess what happened.'

'Calm down, Harry. Happened where?'

'At the RSPCA. You'll never guess.'

'Then why don't you tell me?'

'I rescued a kitten that was stuck in an old pipe.'

'Did you now?' his dad said. 'Well done, son,'

He was facing the window that looked out on the street although he couldn't see out. A blast had blinded him during the last year of the Second World War, eight years before Harry was born.

'It was covered in so much mud you'd never have guessed it was a ginger, I mean marmalade, kitten. Mr Jenner said it would have died if it wasn't for me.'

Harry's dad nodded and Harry took a big breath. It was time for the big question.

'Mr Jenner said I could keep the kitten if I wanted to. Only I'd need permission from my mum and dad. Dad, can I keep him? He's so soft and he's funny too. He loves the water. If you could only see him . . .'

As he said the word 'see', his dad's face wrinkled up and Harry wished he'd used another word, but it was too late now.

'Please, Dad. It wouldn't cost much to feed him.'

But his dad was already shaking his head. 'It'll cost more than we have and what if it's sickly? We can't afford veterinary bills and what if I tread on it by mistake? I could hurt it. No, Harry, I don't think so. Now isn't a good time for a pet and certainly not a vulnerable kitten.'

'But . . .' Harry's mouth fell open. He couldn't believe his dad was really saying no. 'Please . . .'

'I'm sorry, Harry, but that's my final decision.'

Harry could tell by his dad's set face that he meant it.

Harry wanted to shout, 'I hate you!' but he stopped himself. He ran out of the room and up the stairs to his own room. Other children had dads who could see. Other children had dads who would let them have pets. But his dad wouldn't let him have anything. It wasn't fair.

Half an hour later Harry heard his mum come home. Soon after, she called him down for dinner and asked him about his day.

'I rescued a kitten,' he said, half-hoping she might be able to change his dad's mind.

'Did you?' she said. 'Where is it? I love kittens.'

'He's still at the RSPCA centre. I wanted to keep it only Dad said . . .'

'I said he couldn't,' Harry's dad said firmly.

'Oh, that's a shame,' Harry's mum said.

'It's just not practical,' said Harry's dad. 'Not with the way things are.'

'No, I suppose not,' said Harry's mum, but she sounded sad.

'You should have seen him, Mum,' Harry said. 'He was so small. But really brave and he loves water.'

'I would have liked to see him,' Harry's mum told him. 'Very much.'

'You could come to the RSPCA . . .'

'Maybe I will on my day off.'

'Someone might have already adopted him by then,' Harry said, and then he had to swallow hard, because he'd so wanted to be the one to take care of him.

'Remember the smoky grey cat we used to have at St Dunstan's? That cat loved you,' Harry's mum said to his dad as they ate dinner at the small table in the kitchen.

Harry's dad smiled as he shook his head. 'It just loved my pillow. I was forever finding it asleep on top of it. Not a nice surprise when you're a newly blind man.'

'The others were always jealous the cat chose your bed.'

'That wasn't my fault.'

Harry's mum nodded.

'Sometimes animals pick us rather than us choosing them,' she said to Harry.

Harry stirred his food around on his plate, utterly miserable. All he could think about was the little feral kitten that he'd rescued.

'I need to do my homework,' he said, and ran up to his room blinking back tears.

At the RSPCA centre the marmalade kitten woke up on a soft blanket to find himself in a cage with a bowl of water in the corner. Around him he could see other cats in cages. Some of them were asleep, but most were awake. The kitten had never slept by himself before and he missed his mum and his brothers and sisters.

He stood up, stretched and looked out of his cage, looking for the boy who'd been kind to him. But Harry didn't come and the kitten was still very tired. He made a soft, sad sound, scratched at the blanket, curled up and went back to his lonely sleep.

Chapter 7

Mr Jenner was just having his morning cup of tea when Harry arrived at the centre.

'What did your parents say about keeping the kitten?' he asked him.

Harry's voice caught in his throat and he had to swallow hard so that he could speak normally.

'My dad said no,' he said.

'Ah,' nodded Mr Jenner as he took a last slurp of tea. 'That's a shame. But it can't be helped. We'll have to do our best to find another nice new home for the kitten. One where he'll be loved and cherished and given tasty food to eat and played with. Maybe he'll even become Sir Winston Churchill's cat and live at Chartwell.'

'Can I see him?' Harry asked.

'Of course. I'll come with you,' Mr Jenner said, putting his tea cup down. 'He's a lot more lively than the last time you saw him. Amazing how animals bounce back with a bit of food and drink and a good rest.'

The marmalade kitten certainly didn't look like he had been stuck in a rusty pipe only the day before, and was barely recognizable from when Harry had first found him covered in thick mud. Now his ginger coat shone and his chest and four pure-white paws were as white as could be.

When Harry stopped next to his cage the kitten came running over, looked up at him, purred and put out his paw.

'I'm sorry you can't come home with me,'
Harry said, pushing his fingers through the
bars for the kitten to sniff and lick at.

He felt like his heart was breaking and he
wished the kitten could be his more than
anything in the world.

'You can get him out if you like,' Mr Jenner
said. 'Kittens and cats need to be regularly
stroked if they're to make good pets. I'll be
back once I've seen to the dogs. They haven't
had their breakfast yet and will soon start
barking to let me know.'

Harry pulled back the small bolt that kept
the cat cage doors closed and the kitten ran
straight into his lap. The tiny cat rubbed his
furry marmalade head against Harry's hand
and purred and purred.

Harry stroked the kitten and then pulled out
his shoelace from his shoe and wiggled it in
front of the kitten for him to play with.

The kitten watched the wiggling thing trying to escape along the floor and then he pounced on it.

'Just like a lion chasing a cobra,' Harry told him.

When the kitten had had enough of the chasing game he climbed up Harry's jumper sleeve and nestled in the spot where Harry's neck joined his shoulder, purring. The kitten's fur tickled Harry's neck, but Harry didn't mind. He liked it.

'Better be getting off to school, hadn't you, Harry,' Mr Jenner said, when he came back. 'You don't want to be late.'

Harry looked up at the clock on the wall. It was almost nine!

'I'll be back after school,' he called out as he ran off, leaving Mr Jenner to give the kitten his breakfast.

*

The bell was ringing as Harry cycled through the school gates. He jumped off his bike and put it next to William's in the bike rack. He was breathing hard as he ran into class and sat down next to his friend.

'Why're you so late?' William asked him.

'Had to visit the kitten I rescued last night,' Harry said, as the teacher came into the room.

Today there was a quiz to identify when some of Winston Churchill's most famous speeches were made.

'What about this one?' Miss Dunbar asked the class: '"We shall defend our island, whatever the cost may be. We shall fight on the beaches. We shall fight on the landing grounds. We shall fight in the fields, and in the streets, we shall fight in the hills; we shall never surrender."'

Lots of the class knew the answer and put their hands up, but Harry wasn't in the mood to answer questions, especially not about Winston Churchill. If there hadn't been a war then his dad would still be able to see. He'd be the same as other dads. He might have let him keep the kitten because he wouldn't have been worried about standing on him by mistake.

'Jenny?'

'After Dunkirk.'

'And which year was that?'

'June 1940.'

'Well done. How about this one,' Miss Dunbar asked: '"Never in the field of human conflict was so much owed by so many to so few."'

'Battle of Britain,' William said.

They'd learnt about the start of the war in 1939 and how at first it had seemed there was no need to worry about bombs or to evacuate the children to the countryside. Then Winston Churchill became Prime Minister in 1940 and the war really began as far as Britain was concerned. After five more long years and countless battles, the war in Europe ended on VE day on the 8 May 1945. The grenade that blinded Harry's dad was thrown only a few weeks before.

Chapter 8

When Harry ran out of the cattery, the marmalade kitten tried to wriggle out of Mr Jenner's hands and run after him. But Mr Jenner didn't let him go.

'Oh, no you don't,' he said. 'Harry will be back after school. Now, how about some breakfast?'

The kitten looked up at Mr Jenner and Mr Jenner stroked his furry head before popping him back in his cage while he went to make up some kitten formula and put a little bit of fish on a separate plate. The kitten looked so young that he wasn't sure if it could manage solid food yet, but he hoped so.

First Harry had gone and now the man had left him too. The little kitten pushed at the door to his cage, but it didn't open. He tried again and gave the bar a bite with his sharp kitten teeth. But he couldn't get out and even though he gave a little cry, Harry didn't come back to play with him.

The marmalade kitten climbed up the bars of his cage until he reached the top where they had wider spaces between them. Spaces that were large enough for a small kitten to squeeze himself through.

In just a few seconds he was out and he nimbly jumped down from the top of the cage on to the ground and set off out of the cattery as the rest of the cats watched.

'Here we are,' Mr Jenner said, coming back from the kitchen with the marmalade kitten's breakfast. But the kitten wasn't there.

The kitten sniffed the air. He noticed that the dogs' kennels smelt different to the cattery as he wandered in to them. The dogs inside immediately became very alert at the sight of him. A yellow Labrador stood up and wagged her tail. She sniffed through the bars of her cage at the kitten and the kitten sniffed back. Other dogs were more wary and didn't come close. One went to the back of his cage as far away from the kitten as he could get. Another started barking and then other dogs barked too.

The kitten gave a cry and hid behind a sack of dog biscuits as Mr Jenner came running in.

'What's going on?' he shouted to the dogs. 'Hush now, hush!'

When the dogs had finally calmed down, Mr Jenner spotted the kitten over by the dog biscuits.

'Well, what on earth are you doing there?' he said, as he scooped the trembling kitten up. 'Your breakfast's waiting for you through here. You can't eat dog biscuits.'

The yellow Labrador whined as they left the kennels and the kitten looked back at her and gave a miaow.

Mr Jenner put the kitten back in its cage and it lapped up the kitten formula and then it ate up the chopped fish as well.

Once his tummy was full the kitten had a nap on the soft blanket in his cage, while Mr Jenner went off to see to the two budgerigars and one canary they had staying with them.

An hour later the kitten woke up from his nap and was ready to explore again.

Mr Jenner had made sure the door to the kitten's cage was securely locked when he'd put him back in it. But the kitten didn't even try going out the front way. Instead he climbed up the cage bars as he'd done before and squeezed his way out. This time he went in the opposite direction to the one in which the kennels with the noisy dogs had been.

In the RSPCA reception room there were lots of interesting smells from the different people and animals that had been there for a kitten to sniff at. A spider on the wall made a tasty, but small, snack. Climbing the bookcase with boxes of files on it was no problem at all for a nimble kitten and Mr Jenner's woollen scarf made a perfect bed to sleep in when he got tired of playing with it.

Chapter 9

As soon as school was over Harry cycled back to the RSPCA centre. But when he got to the kitten's cage the door was closed, but the kitten wasn't there.

'Where is he?' Harry asked, running back to Mr Jenner, who was seeing to the dogs. Surely the kitten hadn't gone to a new home already?

'Oh, he hasn't got out again, has he?' Mr Jenner said. 'That's the third time today. I found him by the dog biscuit bag a little while after you'd left this morning, he does seem to be used to eating solid food which is good but I didn't want him eating dog biscuits. Then I found him on my desk in the reception area asleep on my scarf. I don't even know how he managed to get out of his cage. None of the other cats and kittens have done so.'

'He's like a Little Houdini,' Harry said.

'That's a good name for him,' Mr Jenner laughed.

Behind him Harry heard a miaow and when he looked round there was the kitten staring up at him. Harry crouched down and picked him up. He was so light and so soft.

'Maybe he was just searching for you,' Mr Jenner said with a smile.

'Hello, Little Houdini,' said Harry.

Little Houdini rubbed his face against Harry's face and Harry laughed.

'Mr Colville wasn't in when I called his office,' Mr Jenner told Harry. 'But his secretary said as far as she knew he hadn't found a marmalade cat and would we be able to deliver the kitten ourselves. I said of course we would.'

Harry's heart sank.

'When does he have to go?' he asked.

'Sir Winston Churchill's birthday is on the 30 November,' Mr Jenner said.

'Tomorrow!'

That was no time at all.

'He'll be eighty-eight years old,' Mr Jenner added.

Harry frowned as he stroked Little Houdini. That was far too old to look after a lively kitten like Little Houdini. Plus Harry wasn't even sure if the ex-prime minister could walk. Sir Winston Churchill had broken his thigh in Monte Carlo in the summer and been flown home in an ambulance. It had been in all the papers and on the television. Harry didn't know how long it would take for someone's thigh to heal but he was sure that having a kitten like Little Houdini around wouldn't help.

What if Sir Winston lost him? Harry didn't want Little Houdini to get stuck in another pipe, or maybe even stuck in something worse, not if Harry wasn't there to rescue him.

Harry bit his bottom lip as he imagined poor Little Houdini wandering along a snowy road trying to get back to Harry, lost and all alone in the cold. And suddenly Harry knew he couldn't let Little Houdini go to Sir Winston. He just couldn't.

'The kitten has such a good relationship with you that I think it'd be best if you took him to Chartwell on your bike tomorrow,' Mr Jenner said.

Harry nodded but inside he was screaming: 'No no no!' He would never let Little Houdini go.

'I'll see you here about eight then when you come to pick him up,' Mr Jenner told Harry, when one of the dogs started barking and then the others joined in.

Little Houdini rubbed his face against Harry's hands.

'I'd better see what's wrong in there,' Mr Jenner said, and he hurried off to the kennels.

Almost without thinking what he was doing, as if he were someone else doing it, Harry carried Little Houdini to the exit door.

'Night, Harry!' Mr Jenner called from the door to the kennels.

'Night!' Harry called back without turning round.

Little Houdini miaowed as Harry ran to his bicycle and put the kitten in the basket. If Mr Jenner saw what he was doing he'd be in so much trouble. But Sir Winston Churchill couldn't love the kitten as much as Harry would love him. No one could.

Casting one final nervous glance behind him, Harry pushed down on the pedal and cycled out of the yard.

Chapter 10

'Hello, son,' Harry's dad called out as Harry tried to sneak into the house with the kitten. 'You're back early.'

His dad was in the lounge, sitting in his usual chair.

'Hello,' Harry replied and Little Houdini gave a meow.

Harry pretended to cough to disguise the sound as he ran up the stairs holding the kitten.

He pushed open the door to his box room bedroom and went inside. As soon as he put him on the floor Little Houdini tugged with his sharp kitten teeth at the tassels on the edge of the threadbare rug in the centre of the room. When he'd had enough of doing that he went to explore under the bed.

Harry was feeling sick. He knew he shouldn't have taken the kitten but it was too late now. He'd done it.

He tore out a page from one of his exercise books and scrunched up the paper into a ball and rolled it along the carpet. Little Houdini immediately came out from under the bed, chased after it and pounced on the paper before rolling on to his back with the ball in his paws. Harry couldn't help laughing because the little kitten looked so funny but he laughed softly because he didn't want his dad to hear.

One of Harry's jobs at the RSPCA was to refill the animals' water bowls.

'It's very important that they have fresh water,' Mr Jenner had told him. 'Cats and dogs and birds can't tell us when they're thirsty so we need to make sure there's always a drink ready for them where they are.'

Sometimes Mr Jenner also let him help put the food in the animals' food bowls.

'A healthy appetite is a sign of a healthy pet,' Mr Jenner always said.

Most of all Harry liked stroking the cats and taking the dogs, especially Callie, for a walk.

Harry bit his bottom lip as he thought that after today Mr Jenner probably wouldn't let him help at the RSPCA any more and that made him sad. But Little Houdini needed him.

'Back in a minute,' Harry told Little Houdini as he headed out of the room to fetch him a bowl of water.

*

When he'd gone Little Houdini looked at the door Harry had gone out of. He didn't want to be left on his own. He wanted to play with Harry.

Harry had pulled the door to but the kitten only needed a very small space to squeeze through.

Once he was in the hallway he went into Harry's parents' room and jumped up on to the bed. Harry wasn't there but the kitten found a ball of wool at the side of the bed to play with and for a few minutes he forgot all about Harry.

'You all right, son?' Harry's dad asked him as Harry headed down the passage and into the kitchen.

'Fine,' Harry said.

He took a bowl from the cupboard, filled it with water and headed back upstairs, but when he got to his room he couldn't see the kitten anywhere.

'Little Houdini,' he hissed as he looked under the bed. 'Little Houdini, where are you?'

He searched all round his room and in the cupboard and the chest of drawers with a deepening sense of dread. The kitten had gone.

Harry went out of his room and looked down the stairs. Could Little Houdini have got down them? The marmalade kitten was very small, but he was also very determined and brave. Harry was pretty sure that Little Houdini would have been able to get down the stairs if he'd wanted to. He bit his bottom lip. He shouldn't have left the kitten alone.

Harry went down the stairs and into the lounge. His dad was sitting in the armchair he always sat in, but now he had Little Houdini on his lap.

When the kitten saw Harry, he jumped off the chair and ran to him, miaowing.

'Is that the kitten you were telling me about?' Harry's dad asked him. 'He's so soft.'

'Yes,' Harry said.

'But what's he doing here? You know you can't keep him.'

'I know. It's just . . . I couldn't bear . . . Mr Jenner didn't see me . . .'

Harry's dad's face looked shocked.

'You didn't steal him?'

'Yes,' Harry choked out the words as the tears streamed down his face. His dad wouldn't understand. 'I'll take him to Chartwell in the morning.'

'Chartwell?' His dad sounded confused.

'He's supposed to be Sir Winston Churchill's birthday present.'

'Oh, Harry.' Now his dad sounded really disappointed. 'He has to go to him then. Everyone owes him so much.'

But Harry didn't agree.

'He's the reason you're blind,' he said.

'No, Harry. Sir Winston Churchill's the reason Britain's free,' Harry's dad said. 'I don't blame him for my injury. Death and injuries are what happens in war. But I'd go again. I'd fight for Sir Winston and Great Britain, even knowing that I'd be blinded I'd still fight for our freedom because freedom is more important than one person's troubles.'

Harry hadn't thought about it like that before.

'I'm sorry, Dad,' he said. 'I know it was wrong. It's just that Sir Winston's so old and Little Houdini's so young and adventurous. But I'll take him to Chartwell in the morning.'

'Good lad,' said his dad.

But Harry felt miserable. He still didn't want to give Little Houdini away.

'You know,' his dad said softly, 'if he were my kitten, I'd give him so many cuddles tonight that it'd be enough to last him a lifetime.'

Harry sniffed back his tears and looked over at Little Houdini who was trying to climb up the curtains.

'He does love to play and have cuddles,' he said as he lifted the kitten down.

'I think we've got some leftover fish in the larder he can have for his supper,' Harry's dad said. 'He'll be a nice surprise for your mum when she gets home from the night shift in the morning.'

'Do you like him, Dad?' Harry asked.

'Of course,' his dad replied, looking sad for a moment. 'But that doesn't mean we can keep him. Or that what you did was right, because it wasn't.'

Harry gave Little Houdini to his dad and a moment later the kitten was climbing up his jumper and resting in his favourite spot – nestled into the crook of a neck.

'I can feel him purring,' said Harry's dad and he smiled.

Suddenly there was a knock at the front door and Harry froze.

'It'll be the police,' he said. 'I shouldn't have taken the kitten.'

Chapter 11

But it wasn't the police. It was Mr Jenner standing there in his RSPCA officer's uniform. He looked worried.

'Little Houdini's missing,' he said. 'I've looked everywhere for him.'

'I'm sorry,' Harry started to say. 'I wasn't thinking. I didn't mean . . .'

Harry's dad came to stand behind him in the narrow hallway. In one hand he held Little Houdini. He rested his other hand on Harry's right shoulder and gave it a reassuring squeeze.

Harry hadn't told Mr Jenner that his dad was blind.

Little Houdini wriggled out of Harry's dad's hand to sit on Harry's left shoulder, next to his neck.

'Harry thought it'd be quicker if he took the kitten to Chartwell straight from here in the morning,' Harry's dad told Mr Jenner.

Harry had never been to Chartwell, although everyone in this part of Kent, and probably everyone in the country, knew it was the home of the famous Sir Winston Churchill, when he wasn't in London.

Harry looked up at his dad covering for him and thought how lucky he was to have a dad that would do that.

'I shouldn't have taken him,' Harry said to Mr Jenner. 'I'm sorry.'

'Well, you are right. It will be less of a trip in the bicycle basket for Little Houdini from your house to Chartwell than from the RSPCA centre,' Mr Jenner said. 'I just wished you'd told me what you were planning.'

'I'm sorry,' Harry said again and he really was.

'But what about food for him?' Mr Jenner asked.

'We've got some fish from last night,' Harry's dad said and Mr Jenner nodded.

'He'll like that.'

'Would you like to come in for a cup of tea?' Harry's dad asked Mr Jenner. But Mr Jenner said he had to be getting back.

'Another time maybe. I'm always here,' Harry's dad said.

'Yes. I will,' said Mr Jenner. 'I expect Harry's told you I used to train guide dogs before I worked for the RSPCA.'

'He didn't mention it, but I'd be very interested to hear about it,' Harry's dad said.

'I've often wondered what it would be like to have a guide dog and how much difference one would really make.'

Harry stared up at his dad in amazement. He'd never mentioned guide dogs before.

'Oh, believe me they make an incredible difference. We've got a dog at the RSPCA centre, Callie, who'd be just perfect.'

Mr Jenner turned and headed back down the path, but then he stopped.

'Oh – before I forget – I brought this for you, Harry.' He pulled a badge from his pocket. 'I meant to give it to you this morning when you came before school. You certainly deserve it for saving Little Houdini.'

He handed Harry an Animal Defenders badge.

Harry stared at the badge, feeling guilty, and not sure if he really deserved it or not. The badge had a silver cat, dog and a horse embossed on the front and the words 'Animal Defender' engraved around it. He'd never be allowed to be an Animal Defender again if Mr Jenner knew he'd meant to kidnap Little Houdini. But he'd definitely been trying to defend an animal.

'Th – thank you,' Harry said.

He gave the badge to his dad to feel.

'Careful of the pin.'

His dad turned the badge round and round in his hands, a gentle smile on his face, before he gave it back to Harry.

'Thank you, Mr Jenner,' Harry said.

'You've got a fine boy there, Mr Jones,' Mr Jenner told Harry's dad.

'Yes, I have,' his dad said, smiling. 'Make sure you come back for that cup of tea.'

'I will.'

Little Houdini licked at Harry's neck with his raspy tongue and yawned.

Chapter 12

It was dawn when Harry woke up and looked over at Little Houdini asleep on his pillow. As if he knew he was being watched, the little kitten opened his bright blue eyes and stared back at Harry.

'Harry,' Harry's mum said from the other side of the door. 'Harry, can I come in?'

Harry jumped out of bed with Little Houdini right behind him. He picked the little kitten up before he opened the door in case he went running out.

'Oh, isn't he adorable,' Harry's mum said when she saw the kitten, and she gave Little Houdini a stroke.

Little Houdini purred and then wriggled out of Harry's hands and quick as a flash jumped on to Harry's mum's shoulder and sat purring next to her neck.

'He loves doing that,' Harry said.

'And I love him doing it!' Harry's mum squeaked.

After breakfast it was time to take Little Houdini to Chartwell. Harry wasn't looking forward to it, but it had to be done. He pinned his new RSPCA Animal Defender badge to his coat lapel.

His mum handed him her woolly scarf.

'Put this in the bicycle basket with Little Houdini so he won't get too cold on the journey,' she said. 'And make sure you wrap up well too and be careful on your bike. It's icy out there.'

'Thanks, Mum,' Harry said, as he and Little Houdini headed to the door.

'Say happy birthday to Sir Winston from me,' his dad called after them.

Harry didn't answer because he didn't think he could do that. His mum kissed him on the top of his head and gave Little Houdini one last stroke.

'See you later,' she said.

Harry wished he could keep pushing the squeaky bicycle pedals up the steep incline of Hosey Hill for ever and never reach Chartwell. Little Houdini curled up on the scarf in the bicycle basket and barely moved during the icy-cold journey.

But all too soon they'd reached the trees at the edge of the estate and Harry was cycling through the huge wooden gates. Ahead of him lay a grand red-brick mansion – Sir Winston Churchill's home.

Harry had never even seen a house as big as this one before. It was much larger than his school and that could fit more than 200 children and the teachers in it.

'Well, you'll have lots of places to explore in there,' he told Little Houdini.

Little Houdini looked up at him and gave a miaow.

'Beautiful, isn't it?' a man on a bicycle behind him said and Harry nodded.

He hadn't expected to find other people there waiting with gifts for Sir Winston Churchill's birthday. But there were. Lots of people wrapped up against the cold and lots of gifts.

'I've made him one of my cakes . . .'

'Cyclamen from the garden.'

Little Houdini stood up on his back legs with his front paws resting on the front of the wicker basket and looked out.

'Can't beat an apple pie made with the best Kent apples from the orchard . . .'

'Did you hear about the boy who brought Winston some goldfish one year? They're still in the pond now. Grew to be huge.'

The postman arrived with a bulging sack full of birthday cards.

'Parcels are coming in the other van,' he said. 'Including a case of champagne.'

Harry and Little Houdini joined the end of the queue of people with presents. As they waited Harry imagined how impressed William would be when he told him he'd been to Chartwell to deliver Sir Winston Churchill's birthday present. But then that thought made him sad because Little Houdini wouldn't be his kitten any more.

A woman arrived with a miniature black poodle puppy and it started to bark excitedly at the people who were waiting. Not that anyone was frightened. The puppy was very small. But Little Houdini didn't like the barking. It was like the scary dogs that barked at him before. He jumped out of the bicycle basket and went running off across the frosty grass.

He was so fast that for a second Harry didn't realize he'd gone.

'No, wait! Come back!' Harry shouted, as he went running after the kitten. 'Little Houdini!'

Chapter 13

The kitten hid under a large rosemary bush close to the footpath. Harry didn't see him when he ran past, but Little Houdini saw Harry's legs. He gave a miaow but Harry didn't hear him.

'Little Houdini, Little Houdini!' Harry called out in panic as he carried on running. If he didn't find the kitten then Mr Jenner and his mum and dad would be so disappointed in him. Not to mention Sir Winston Churchill!

Little Houdini came out from his hiding place and headed after Harry who was running towards a small cottage where an old man with a bald head was working in the front garden.

'Have you seen a kitten?' Harry gasped when he reached the man. 'He ran off when a puppy started barking and I can't find him. But he's only little and he can't have gone far. Although he's very fast.'

The old man grinned, showing the space where his dentures would go once he'd put them in. Harry thought grinning was a bit rude considering how worried he was.

'Would it by any chance be a marmalade kitten?' the old man asked him.

'Yes. How did you know?' Harry said.

The old man gave a soft chuckle and pointed at the ground.

Harry looked behind him and there was Little Houdini looking up at him.

The kitten gave a miaow and Harry breathed a sigh of relief as he scooped him up.

'I'm so glad I found you,' he whispered.

'Looks like it was the other way round and that kitten found you!' the old man said, laughing. 'What's his name?'

'Little Houdini,' Harry told him.

'Ah-ha. Good name. I'm Ned by the way. Most people call me Old Ned nowadays although I started off as just Ned.'

'Harry,' said Harry. 'Harry Jones.'

'That's a fine badge you're wearing, Harry Jones.'

Harry told Old Ned how he'd rescued Little Houdini from the pipe. 'And now he's going to be one of Sir Winston Churchill's birthday presents.'

'Is he indeed? Sir Winston will be pleased. He's got a soft spot for marmalade cats and has had a few of them over the years. Me too.

You can be sure your kitten will have a good life here. Sir Winston loves all animals and he couldn't bear for any of them to be mistreated. Now, how about some tea and a bit of breakfast?'

Harry bit his bottom lip. 'I should be taking Little Houdini to the main house,' he said.

'Oh, don't worry about that yet. They'll still be bringing cards and presents for Winny long after you've eaten. I expect you're hungry. Growing boys are always hungry and I bet Little Houdini wouldn't mind a second breakfast either.'

Harry didn't really like tea, but he was hungry and he didn't want to be rude. Old Ned put three sugars in his cup and it didn't taste too bad.

Little Houdini darted around the kitchen exploring every nook and cranny. He put his nose to the bottom of Old Ned's stove. There was something interesting scuttling around under there that wouldn't come out. Little Houdini lay down to watch it.

'Crumpets. Do you like crumpets, Harry?' Old Ned asked him.

'Yes,' Harry said eagerly. He didn't just like crumpets, he loved them! Although they very rarely had them at home.

'Good,' said Old Ned as he gave Harry some crumpets to toast on the fire with a toasting fork while he chopped up some cooked chicken for Little Houdini.

'Most marmalade cats are very friendly,' Old Ned said, as he put the saucer down close to the kitten. 'Mellow's the word people often use to describe them.'

Little Houdini stopped watching the mouse to eat the chicken, but he looked over at the bottom of the stove every now and again just in case it came out.

'I had my first marmalade kitten when I was younger than you,' Old Ned said. 'It was about the same time as I met Sir Winston, or Winny, as he used to call himself then. When he was a boy his hair was a marmalade colour just like your kitten. Doesn't have much hair now though,' he said, chuckling. 'Bald, like me.' Old Ned settled himself down in his cosy armchair by the fire, remembering the very first time he had met Winston Churchill. He had no idea then that he would be the future prime minister.

Chapter 14

The year was 1882 and seven-year-old Ned was helping his father to dig up the potatoes in the school's vegetable patch.

Ned loved the feel of the earth beneath his fingers and seeing the potato plants bloom. They'd planted the seed potatoes a few months ago and now they were ready to harvest.

'We need to get up as many potatoes as we can before the heavy frosts come,' Ned's dad said, and he headed off with the heavy wheelbarrow full of freshly dug potatoes to the school kitchen. 'Back in a minute.'

Ned carried on digging but stopped when he thought he heard a sniff. He looked round but couldn't see anyone and turned back to his digging thinking he must have imagined it. But only a couple of minutes later, there was the sniff again, louder than before. This time when Ned looked around, he spotted a small ginger-haired boy half hidden in the bushes.

'Hey – you there!' he called out.

The small ginger-haired boy was wearing the uniform of St George's School at Ascot where Ned's dad worked. Pupils weren't allowed over this way. Ned didn't go to the private boarding school; he went to a day school in the village and spent most of his free time helping his dad.

The boy didn't reply and so Ned headed over and grabbed him by the arm.

'What are you doing here?' he said roughly, and then stopped when he saw his face.

The boy, who looked about the same age as him, had grey streaks across his cheeks from the tears that had run down and been quickly wiped away by grubby fingers.

'How old are you?' Ned asked in a softer voice.

'Seven years, eleven months and one day,' the boy told him. He couldn't pronounce his s's properly. 'I never wanted to come to this stupid school and now I'd very much like to go home.'

'How long have you been at the school for?' Ned asked him.

'One whole day but that's quite long enough for me to have formed my opinion of it.'

Ned grinned. He didn't much like going to school either.

'What's your name?'

'Winny. What's yours?'

'Ned.'

'I've got a kitty at home,' Winny lisped, pointing at Ned's ginger-and-white-striped kitten. 'I've got lots of pets who'll be missing me and wondering where I've gone.'

'His name's Sergeant Tommy,' Ned said, as he picked the kitten up and gave him to Winny to hold.

'Why did you name him Sergeant?' Winny asked as he rubbed his dirty face in the kitten's soft fur. Sergeant Tommy purred.

'Because one day, when he's grown a little more, he'll be as brave as a soldier and catch lots of rats,' Ned said, because that was what his dad had told him.

'Are there lots of rats here then?' Winny asked, looking around worriedly.

'Loads! But not for much longer with Sergeant Tommy around!' Ned told him. 'Do you want a sandwich? My mum made them and she always puts lots of homemade strawberry jam in them.'

Winny nodded and Ned shared his sandwiches with him until his dad came back with the wheelbarrow and saw the two of them together.

'You'd best be heading back to the school building now,' he told Winny and Winny scurried off looking much happier than when Ned had first met him.

The next time Ned went with his dad to the school garden it wasn't long before Winny turned up too, and the time after that he was waiting for Ned with a smile and a wave.

'Climbed out of the window,' he told Ned.

'He'll be in real trouble if he gets caught,' Ned's dad said when they got home. 'The headmaster of the school's a cruel man and he'll think nothing of using a cane on your friend if he finds out he's broken the school rules.'

Ned didn't want Winny to be in trouble and he took a woolly hat and his old coat with him as a disguise for Winny the next time he went to the school garden.

'No one will look twice at you if you're not wearing your uniform,' he said.

Winny loved the idea and kept the coat and cap in the gardener's shed for whenever he needed it.

He was wearing the cap and coat, even though it was getting a bit too warm to be wearing them, when the piglets arrived from the farm up the road one Saturday in the spring.

'Six!' Winny said happily when he'd counted them.

'They're called Middle Whites,' Ned told him.

One of the piglets was a lot smaller and thinner than all the others.

'What's wrong with him?' Winny asked Ned's dad.

'Nothing. He's just the runt,' Ned's dad told him. 'That's what they call the last piglet to be born. Often they don't survive because they're not as strong as the others and sometimes the sow, that's the . . .'

'Mother,' Winny interrupted. 'A lady pig is called a sow,' he said, eager to share his animal knowledge.

'Well, sometimes she hasn't got enough to feed all the piglets and she has to make a hard decision, and the runt gets left out.'

'You mean it doesn't get fed?' Winny said, his eyes wide. 'Just because it's the smallest?'

'It's just nature. Just what happens some-times,' Ned's dad told him kindly.

But Winny's head was shaking fast and so was Ned's.

'I'll never EVER let that happen to this one,' Winny said, and he threw his arms round the squealing and surprised runt of a piglet, not caring that he was getting his disguise coat covered in mud and manure.

'I brought Piggly some sugar from the breakfast table,' Winny told Ned the next morning, pulling sugar lumps from his pocket. 'I bet he'll eat these. Come on, little Piggly, come on.'

And the little piglet did manage to eat the first sugar lump and then the second and the third, fourth and fifth.

Winny laughed and laughed when the little piglet nuzzled his pocket to see if there were any more.

He gave the piglet a kiss on the snout and promised to bring him some more the very next day.

Over the next few weeks Piggly spent very little time in the field with the other piglets because

Winny and Ned were too busy playing with him every chance they got.

'Sit, Piggly, sit,' Winny said, holding up his arm and as Piggly looked up at the piece of apple, he automatically sat down. 'Good Piggly!'

'He's as easy to teach as a puppy!' Ned laughed. 'Maybe even easier.'

Fortunately Piggly liked all sorts of vegetables and fruits and even the odd flower or two from the flower garden, which he really wasn't supposed to have, so they had lots of treats to tempt him.

'Can you fetch my ball, Piggly?' Winny asked him, and he threw his ball across the grass. But Piggly was too busy eating some daisies to pay any attention to a ball.

When the other piglets were sent away, Piggly had grown so much that he was sent too.

'Where's he gone?' Winny asked Ned's dad.

'Gone to market,' Ned's dad said.

'Get him back,' Winny begged. 'I'll give you my pocket money to buy him.'

But Ned's dad shook his head. 'It's too late for that.'

'But what will happen to him?'

Ned's dad shook his head. 'The pigs are reared to be eaten, you know that,' he said. 'Don't you?'

Ned began to cry, but Winny looked fierce.

'When I grow up,' Winny said, 'I'm going to have Middle White pigs that will never be sent to market, I promise.'

'And so am I,' Ned told him, sniffing back his tears.

Chapter 15

Harry looked over at Old Ned sitting in the worn armchair. He wasn't sure if the elderly man had fallen asleep or not. Old Ned's bald head was lowered to his chest and Harry couldn't see if his eyes were open or closed.

But then Old Ned muttered to himself, clearly half-asleep. 'Winston's school report said he would never amount to much. How wrong could they be!'

Little Houdini went over to the old man, hopped up on to his lap and pushed his head against his hand for a stroke.

'Oh, hello there,' Old Ned said sleepily. 'Must have dozed off a bit.' He gave the kitten a stroke. 'You remind me of a kitten I used to have called Sergeant Tommy.'

'Crumpets are done,' Harry told him.

'Good. Put lots of butter on them,' Old Ned said. 'They're best with lots of butter.'

Harry spread them with lots of butter and smiled as he bit into his crumpet. Old Ned was right. Lots of butter was best.

'I'd better be getting back up to the main house,' Harry said when they'd finished eating. He didn't want to keep Sir Winston waiting.

'People will be arriving with presents for Winny all day,' Old Ned said. 'One year he was given a lion that he called Rota and another year an albino kangaroo was sent all the way from Australia. Winny wanted to keep the kangaroo in the orchard here but it just wasn't practical.

'When he turned eighty though, now that was a big birthday year. Present after present. Everyone wanted to say thank you for his part in the Second World War. But Winny wouldn't take all the credit. He said the whole nation had the lion's heart but he had the luck to be given the roar. He meant that the whole country had been very brave.'

Harry thought about his dad. He'd been brave, very brave. He'd fought in the war and said he'd fight again even if he knew he'd be blinded by it. His dad had a lion's heart and Harry was proud of him.

'Winston's presents over the years would fill all the rooms in Chartwell ten times over,' Old Ned continued.

Harry thought that Sir Winston got given so many presents that he really didn't need to have Little Houdini as well.

Little Houdini tried to push his paw under the stove to catch the mouse.

'I'll come with you to the main house,' Old Ned said, standing up and putting his cap on.

Little Houdini looked back at the stove and miaowed as Harry picked him up.

'Winny bought the farm next to here, you know, so he could keep pigs, and other animals. But the pigs were his favourites. "Dogs look up to you. Cats look down on you. But a pig looks you in the eye," he used to say.

'The pigs we kept here were more like pets than farm animals. They'd follow me around when I was doing my work. Curious about what I was doing. I'd talk to them all the time and they'd make little grunting sounds as if they could understand every word. Perhaps they could.'

Chapter 16

Harry held Little Houdini as he followed Old Ned across the closely cropped grass of the terrace lawn.

Before them on the hill loomed the huge red-brick mansion of Chartwell. It had lead latticed windows and magnolia growing up the walls.

Harry wondered if Sir Winston was in one of the upstairs rooms, looking out, wondering what Harry and Little Houdini were doing on his lawn.

He tried to hold Little Houdini more tightly in his arms, hiding him from view in case he spoiled the surprise.

They were almost at the house when a horse and cart piled high with baskets of apples, wrapped in newspaper, came clipping through the gates driven by a wrinkled man wearing a checked scarf.

Little Houdini wriggled in Harry's arms but Harry didn't let him go.

'It's all right,' he said. 'I'll look after you.'

'Hey, Ned,' the man driving the horse cart called out. 'How are you?'

'Fine,' Old Ned said. 'And yourself, Jim?'

'Can't complain. Got a load of apples here for Sir Winston's birthday. The animals love them. My Dorrie here will be having a few to say thank you for bringing me here.'

He took a newspaper-wrapped apple from one of the baskets, unwrapped it, and gave it to Harry.

'You can feed her one now if you like.'

'Why's it wrapped in newspaper?' Harry asked.

'Best way of storing them after they've been picked. Last for months in newspaper,' Jim told him.

As Jim spoke, Dorrie sniffed at Little Houdini and Little Houdini miaowed and sniffed back. As Harry fed the rosy apple to the horse, Little Houdini sniffed at that too and Harry laughed.

'Kitten don't eat apples,' he told him.

'Not unless they're very hungry,' Jim said. 'And even then I don't know if they would. But then I'd never have thought I'd see a horse eating its own blanket if I hadn't seen it with my own eyes during the First World War. All the ponies and horses I've had since then have been on the plump side because I feed them up. I can't get the image of those skinny beasts out of my head. They worked so hard for us and we couldn't even feed them properly.'

Old Ned shook his head. 'Terrible time for everyone,' he said. 'And unthinkable what those animals went through. Thank goodness Sir Winston was able to get the Ministry of Shipping to bring more of them back.'

Harry stroked Dorrie's neck and she shook her mane.

'The government was only getting a few thousand horses back a week until Winny weighed in and made a big fuss. Then it went up to 9,000.'

'Far too many of them suffered,' Jim told Harry. 'War's no place for animals. I'm glad we didn't use them so much in the Second World War.'

'My grandad was a soldier in the First World War,' Harry said. He'd seen a photo of him sitting on a horse but he'd never met him because his grandad had been killed at the Front.

'Sir Winston fought in that one too, but not on a horse. He was an infantry officer for the Royal Scots Fusiliers for two years,' Jim said.

'Winston's always been fond of horses. Used to say there's something about the outside of a horse that makes the inside of a man happy,' Old Ned added.

Dorrie whinnied and Jim laughed and unwrapped another apple and gave it to Harry to give to her. 'Dorrie's grandad was one of the horses that went to war and came home again thanks to Sir Winston,' he said.

When Dorrie had finished her apple she clipped on down the driveway with Little Houdini watching her as she went.

Chapter 17

Harry had never been in a house as majestic as Chartwell and he was feeling nervous as well as excited. William would never believe him when he told him about it on Monday.

He, Harry Jones, was actually at Sir Winston Churchill's house, about to go inside.

'We'll go in through the side door,' Old Ned said, looking at Harry's awestruck face staring at the imposing front door with ornate wooden pillars around it.

Harry gave a sigh of relief.

'Grace,' Old Ned called as he opened the smaller door, which had a cat flap in it, at the side of the building. 'Grace, you about?'

But no one came.

'I expect she's busy sorting out all Winny's presents,' Old Ned said. 'I don't know what he'd do without her. She's worked for him for over thirty years. You wait here and I'll be back in a minute.' He pointed to a chair and Harry sat down on it with Little Houdini.

The kitten purred softly as Harry stroked him and soon fell fast asleep. Harry carried on stroking him.

Old Ned had said he wouldn't be long, but when Harry looked up at the clock he saw he'd been waiting for nearly twenty minutes. He bit his bottom lip. Could Old Ned have forgotten about them? He wasn't sure what to do for the best but he decided to wait and hope Ned came back soon.

Little Houdini made soft sounds, stirred and stretched, deep in kitten dreams.

A moment later the outside door opened and in walked an old lady with a lively miniature black poodle puppy.

'This way, Buttons,' the lady said and the puppy looked up at her and wagged its tail.

Little Houdini opened his blue eyes, saw the poodle puppy, gave a yeowl and quick as a flash jumped off Harry's lap on to the tiled floor and ran off down the passage.

'No, Little Houdini! Come back!' Harry shouted.

But the kitten didn't listen to him. He ran through an open door, across the carpet and leapt on to the floral brocade curtains and within no time at all was at the very top of them and looking down.

'Oh dear,' the lady said to Harry back in the passageway. 'I didn't mean to startle your kitten. I've only just been given Buttons today and he's very young and excitable. I'll shut him in this lean-to and help you catch your kitten. My name's Miss Hamblin. Grace Hamblin.'

'Thank you,' Harry said. 'I'm Harry and the kitten's called Little Houdini.'

'Very apt,' Miss Hamblin said, as they hurried down the passageway.

As they looked in the sitting room Harry told Miss Hamblin how he was bringing Little Houdini to Chartwell as one of Sir Winston's birthday presents.

'A man with a Rolls-Royce came to the RSPCA centre looking for a new cat.'

'Oh yes, that'd be dear Jock,' Grace said, as she looked under the cushions on the armchairs, but not up at the top of the curtains where Little Houdini was hidden. 'I know him very well. But he isn't here today, dear, and neither is Sir Winston. He's in London at his Hyde

Park home and there are no plans for him to come home just yet. He broke his thigh, you know, and is still recovering.'

As Harry listened to Grace he squeezed his hands into fists and dug his nails into his palms to stop himself from cheering. He didn't want Sir Winston to be injured, but he did want to be able to keep Little Houdini for a little while longer. It might be weeks, even months, before Sir Winston came home and Little Houdini could stay with him, maybe even at Harry's house, if Mr Jenner let him and his dad didn't mind. He didn't think his dad would mind now he'd met the kitten and seen how nimble he was. His dad would never be able to step on him by mistake, even if he tried to, because Little Houdini would just hop out of the way as soon as he saw his foot coming.

'Grace!' Old Ned called out from the hallway. 'Grace, where are you?'

Harry and Miss Hamblin hurried out of the room and didn't hear Little Houdini miaowing.

'I've been looking everywhere for you,' Old Ned said.

Little Houdini stared down at the floor from the top of the curtains. It had been fairly easy to get up them, but he wasn't at all sure about how to get down. He stretched out a paw and then quickly brought it back.

'I was taking my present from Sir Winston for a walk,' Miss Hamblin told Ned proudly. 'His name is Buttons because of his button-brown eyes and he's a miniature poodle puppy just like the two Rufuses were. Only he barked at Little Houdini . . .'

'And Little Houdini went running off,' Harry said.

'He really is a bit of an escape artist, isn't he?' Old Ned said. 'I'll help you look for him.'

Buttons didn't like being shut in the lean-to. He scratched at the door and barked and whined to be let out.

Harry felt sorry for the little puppy left all by himself.

'It's not fair to leave him for too long,' he said.

'Poor Buttons does sound really distressed,' Miss Hamblin agreed and they headed back down the passageway to let the puppy out.

Buttons was overjoyed to see them. He raced out of the lean-to as soon as the door was opened, stood up on his back legs and put his front paws on Ned's shins, then ran over to Miss Hamblin and Harry, wagging his tail very fast.

'You can help us find Little Houdini,' Old Ned told him.

'But don't frighten the kitten again,' warned Miss Hamblin.

Harry crouched down and the puppy climbed on to his lap and licked his face.

'He's so lovely,' Harry smiled, as he gave Buttons's curly black coat a stroke.

'And smart too, or so he will be if he's anything like the last two poodles that lived here,' Miss Hamblin said. 'Sir Winston bought Buttons for me because he thought I'd be as upset as he was when his own second miniature poodle, dear Rufus 2 died. And he was right, I was very upset. I used to take both Rufuses around St James's Park for walks and I'd grown quite attached even though I'm more of a cat person than a dog one.' As she spoke Buttons came over to her and she picked him up and cuddled him to her.

Harry thought that Miss Hamblin was both a cat and a dog person. He didn't see why anyone had to be one or the other.

'Winston said Rufus was starting to love me more than him, but that wasn't true,' Grace said, chuckling. 'The first Rufus was a great comfort to Winston during the Second World War and he was always so happy to see Winston. As happy as Winston was to see him!'

And she told Harry all about the little dog.

Chapter 18

'Rufus!'

Rufus knew exactly what he was supposed to do when his name was called: run to the person calling him.

But just because he knew what he was supposed to do didn't mean that he always did it.

There were so many other exciting things to do – so many interesting smells, things to chase and places to explore. He wanted to see the chickens before he went back inside and then he would run down to the fish pond for a long cool drink.

'Rufus – food time!'

Instantly turning back towards the house at the sound of those magic words, the miniature brown poodle raced across the freshly dug vegetable patch and in through the French doors, leaving a trail of muddy paw-prints behind him.

'Oh, there you are at last, Rufus,' said Winston Churchill, who was sitting at the head of the dining table, looking down at Rufus affectionately. 'We've all been waiting for you.'

Rufus panted and wagged his tail as Winston nodded to the butler, and the butler nodded to the maid, who brought in Rufus's full dinner plate and placed it on a cloth on the Persian carpet, next to Winston.

Winston nodded again to the butler and the butler nodded to the maid, who then brought in everyone else's food.

Rufus finished his meal first and looked up at Winston, who was still eating, and gave a hopeful whine.

After lunch Winston liked to work in his bed, sometimes having meetings and dictating to his secretaries from there too. Rufus liked to lie on the bed with him and rest his head on his knee.

But as soon as Winston got ready to go out he raced to the door to show that he wanted to go too. Sometimes Winston took him with him and let him sit on the seat beside him in the car and he stroked the little dog as he looked out of the window.

Usually they only went for short rides in the Humber car. But one day they left the countryside of Kent behind and headed into the centre of London and 10 Downing Street. It was a long drive and Rufus got sleepy and stopped looking out of the window and slept with his head on Winston's leg instead.

The squirrels in St James's Park were just as quick as the ones at Chartwell and, hard as he tried, Rufus couldn't catch any of them. Every day, and sometimes more than once a day, they walked between 10 Downing Street and the War Rooms on King Charles Street. It only took four minutes to walk between them, if you didn't go into St James's Park. But Rufus loved to run round the park chasing the squirrels and the pigeons who were always just a bit too quick for him.

Rufus panted and trembled when the planes screamed as they flew overhead and sometimes they were dropping bombs. His sensitive hearing meant he always knew when the bombs were on their way long before the people did. He'd start whining and then try to find somewhere to hide but he didn't always make it in time.

Miss Hamblin held his lead when they went to visit a bombsite one day. All around them there were collapsed houses and big holes in the road. Rufus sniffed the dusty air that smelt of damp plaster and sneezed. It wasn't easy to cross the uneven rubble-strewn road with holes in it and he yelped as his paw stepped on something sharp.

'There, there, dear,' Mr Churchill said, and he picked him up and carried him.

Rufus was happy to be carried until he saw another dog and then he wriggled to get down so he could say hello.

'Rufus meet Rip,' Winston said, as Rufus wagged his tail and sniffed at the small mixed-breed dog and Rip sniffed and wagged his tail back at him.

'Rip's saved the lives of over a hundred people,' said the man from the PDSA with Rip. 'Not bad for a stray dog I found in a bombed-out building.'

'Indeed,' smiled Winston as he gave Rip a stroke. 'You're a very fine search and rescue dog and deserve a medal for all your hard work.'

'He'd like that, although I think he'd prefer a sandwich,' the man laughed. 'Dripping sandwiches are his favourite.'

Rufus gave a woof because he liked dripping sandwiches too and fortunately the man had brought some with him and shared them with the two dogs and Winston and Grace.

Winston went to visit lots of other bombsites after that but he didn't take Rufus with him again.

'I don't want your paws getting cut on the rubble, dear,' he said.

So Rufus stayed behind and went to the park with Grace and chased the squirrels instead.

And then one day, a long while later, everyone was very excited and Winston was smiling and laughing. Miss Hamblin kept stroking Rufus and saying: 'I can't believe it.'

Mr Churchill gave him a big kiss on the top of his furry head.

'It's over, darling,' he said. 'The war in Europe is finally over.'

The next morning Rufus was given a special bone to celebrate and taken by Grace for an early morning walk in St James's Park. There were lots more people walking in the park than usual and all of them were smiling and some of them were singing and dancing.

'Hello, little doggie,' a man in a sailor's uniform said to Rufus.

'This is the best day ever,' laughed a girl in a green hat.

Rufus looked at a squirrel and gave a woof.

'All right,' Grace said, as she released his lead. 'But you'll have to be quick. This is only supposed to be a little walk. We've got lots to do today.'

As soon as he was free from his lead Rufus chased after the squirrel, but it ran up a tree and looked down at him from one of the high branches. Rufus stood on his back legs and put his front paws on the tree trunk and barked, but the squirrel didn't come down to play.

Back at 10 Downing Street, Winston was so busy shaking people's hands and being clapped on the back that he hardly had time to stroke Rufus. But Rufus didn't mind because everyone was so happy. They laughed and celebrated all night long.

Rufus even got to go to Buckingham Palace and play with a corgi called Susan while people danced and sang in the streets below.

A few days later, Rufus was sitting next to Winston in the Humber car and looking out of the window.

'We're almost there,' Winston said, and his voice sounded excited and that made Rufus excited too. 'Almost at Chartwell.' They'd left the city behind and were out in the countryside. Winston opened the car window and smiled as they drove in through the vast gates and now Rufus was really, really excited.

He began to pant and then to whine as he sniffed at the air. He knew where they were.

'Home,' said Winston.

As soon as the chauffeur opened the rear car door Rufus jumped out and ran off across the grass sniffing all the old familiar smells and racing down to the lake for a long drink of water.

Chapter 19

Little Houdini half climbed and half fell down the brocade curtains and landed on the soft carpet. He'd almost caught up with Harry in the passageway when he saw the excited black poodle puppy, and Buttons saw him too and gave a yap. Quick as a flash Little Houdini turned and ran the other way down the steps to the kitchen.

In the kitchen the kitten found a bowl of puppy food and had a taste of it along with a drink of water from a water bowl.

Scampering towards the next room he found something even more interesting. Hundreds of tiny multicoloured fish swimming about in big tank on top of a large wooden trunk.

Little Houdini hopped up on to the trunk and watched the fish through the glass, his head turning from side to side as they darted about. He put his paw on the glass and miaowed but the little fishes didn't come closer.

Little Houdini looked up at the top of the tank and was just about to jump up on to it when he heard people talking in the room above him and recognized one voice he knew well. Harry!

Little Houdini gave a purr, jumped down from the trunk and ran out of the room and up the stairs to find him, but once again found the barking puppy just ahead of him instead. Buttons looked round and gave a yap.

Scared of the loud noise, Little Houdini ran into the library and hopped up on to the bookshelves looking for a place to hide. There were old children's stuffed toys left in spots where books had been taken out. Little Houdini gnawed on the arm of a grubby panda that was almost as big as him. There wasn't enough room for the panda and Little Houdini to play on the shelves at the same time and the panda landed on the floor with a soft thud.

It was too soft a sound for Harry to hear, but Buttons heard it and looked over at the library door.

'This way, Buttons,' Harry said, leading him the other way.

But Buttons pulled him towards the library, wagging his tail and then he gave another yap.

'Maybe he's trying to tell us something,' Old Ned said, pushing the library door open.

'So many books!' Harry gasped, as he looked up at the bookshelves that went from the floor almost to the ceiling. There was a desk for Sir Winston to work at and comfy red armchairs for reading in.

'Never been in here before,' Old Ned said, staring in awe at the hundreds of books.

Little Houdini looked down from the top shelf where he was now hidden by a stuffed toy giraffe.

'Little Houdini,' Harry called out. 'Little Houdini, are you in here?' He was getting desperate. They had to find him. Where could he be?

Little Houdini's tail twitched. He wanted to go down but he was frightened of Buttons who was staring straight up at him, panting and wagging his tail.

'No sign of your Little Houdini anywhere I'm afraid,' Grace said, coming into the room.

'I left Buttons's food bowl in the kitchen. I wonder if Little Houdini might be hungry and have found it.'

'A cat's sense of smell is fourteen times stronger than a person's,' Harry said. Mr Jenner had told him. 'So he might have done.'

Harry held Buttons's lead as Grace led them down the stairs to the kitchen in the basement.

As soon as Harry had left the library, Little Houdini climbed down from the top of the bookcase. It was much easier than climbing down the curtains. He peeped out of the door and then went after them.

Buttons was very excited to find a half-eaten bowl of food waiting for him in the kitchen and had soon gobbled it all up while Old Ned and Grace looked in cupboards and under the sink for Little Houdini.

'Not in here,' said Grace.

'Not here either,' Old Ned said.

'What if he's stuck somewhere?' Harry said. 'He could be injured.'

'We'll find him,' Old Ned said and Grace nodded.

Harry and Buttons followed Miss Hamblin and Old Ned into the dining room next door and stopped to stare at a painting on the wall of a marmalade cat drinking milk from a saucer on a table while Sir Winston and his wife, who were sitting at the table too, watched. The cat in the painting looked a lot like Harry imagined Little Houdini would look like when he was older.

'Who's that?' Harry asked curiously.

'That's Tango, Winston's cat from many years ago,' Miss Hamblin said. 'As you can see, pets are well treated around here.'

Harry nodded because they certainly did seem to be. Buttons looked up at him and wagged his tail.

'Remember that sky-blue budgerigar Winny had?' Old Ned asked Grace. 'There were a few over the years but some of them were more memorable than others.'

'Toby,' Grace said and they both smiled. 'He was such a character.'

'He used to love sitting on top of my bald head,' Old Ned told Harry as he laughed. 'And more often than not he'd do a whoopsy on it too. I didn't mind too much but some of Winny's other visitors weren't so keen. Winny told them to take it as a compliment!'

Harry would have laughed if he hadn't been so worried about finding Little Houdini. From all the stories he'd heard, Sir Winston certainly seemed to love and spoil his pets.

'He had a special cage in Sir Winston's bedroom and flew round the room, pecking at cabinet papers and sitting on Winston's head . . .' Grace remembered.

'Winston said working in bed with his pets around him was the best way to work,' Grace added. 'And the pets certainly seemed to like it. Toby especially loved it when Winston gave him little bits of black cherry jam and tinned pineapple from his breakfast tray.'

Harry didn't think Little Houdini would like jam or pineapple, but he did think he'd probably like living with Sir Winston here at Chartwell, especially if he had Grace and Old Ned to look after him too. And maybe Harry could come and visit him sometimes. That was if they ever found him!

While Grace and Old Ned carried on talking about the budgie, Harry let go of Buttons's lead and looked round the dining room for Little Houdini. Buttons helped too by sniffing and then licking up the crumbs under the table. Suddenly Buttons gave a woof and ran to the door where Little Houdini stood watching them all.

They all had a little glimpse of the marmalade kitten before he raced away with Buttons yapping behind him.

'Little Houdini!' Harry cried and he, Grace and Old Ned ran after the kitten and the puppy.

Little Houdini headed down the hallway, into the lean-to and out through the cat flap into the crisp, icy-cold air. A speck of something white and cold landed on his head, a moment later there was another white speck, and then more and more. Little Houdini stared up at the sky as more white specks fell from it and swirled around him. Soon he was surrounded by them and he forgot all about finding Harry as he chased after the white specks, desperately trying to catch them.

Buttons was still small enough to squeeze out of the cat flap, although it took him a few tries before he could make it out into the chilly air after Little Houdini, and soon the two animals were racing around together trying to catch the falling snowflakes.

'Oh,' Grace said, and she stopped so quickly that Harry almost bumped into her as she pulled open the door to the terrace. He looked where she was pointing and saw Buttons and Little Houdini playing together in the swirling snow. Friends at last.

Harry, Ned and Grace burst out laughing as Buttons looked over at them, his muzzle covered in snow.

'Buttons!' Grace called and the poodle puppy raced to her as Little Houdini ran to Harry. Harry picked him up and cuddled the little kitten to him.

'I'm so glad I found you,' he said, as the kitten purred and crawled into the warm spot where Harry's shoulder and neck met. Safe at last.

Chapter 20

'Time for some tea and scones to warm us up, don't you agree?' Grace said, as they headed back inside.

'Oh yes please!' said Harry. He couldn't believe his luck. Crumpets and scones all in one day.

'Harry likes at least three sugars in his tea and he needs lots of jam on his scones too,' Old Ned said.

'And what about you, Ned? How do you like your tea and scones?' Grace asked him.

'Same as Harry, please,' Old Ned said and Grace laughed.

'Just the way I like them too,' she said with a grin. 'Sugary tea and scones with lashings of jam coming right up.'

Harry was just biting into his second scone when he looked through the window and was astonished to see Mr Jenner and his dad outside. They made their way through the snow over to the glass door that Grace quickly opened for them.

'Mr Colville's office phoned,' Mr Jenner said to Harry. 'They made a mistake. A marmalade cat had already been found at another RSPCA centre for Sir Winston's birthday present.'

'So he doesn't want Little Houdini after all?' Harry said, hardly able to believe it. 'But what will happen to Little Houdini now?' He looked down at the kitten who stared back up at him with his big blue eyes. If Little Houdini lived at Chartwell he would at least have been well looked after and Harry might have been able to visit him sometimes. Now he might never see Little Houdini again.

'Well, we think we've found him another home,' Mr Jenner said, smiling.

'Oh' said Harry, his heart sinking. 'Who with?'

'With us,' his dad said with a big grin. 'If you'd still like him?'

Harry's mouth fell open. Little Houdini might really be his to keep for ever. He felt like all his birthdays had come at once.

'You mean it?' he said.

'Yes, I do,' Harry's dad said, and Harry ran to him and hugged him.

'Thank you.'

'Have a scone,' Ned told Harry's dad as he spread one thickly with strawberry jam while Grace poured Mr Jenner a cup of tea.

'I can hardly believe I'm actually in Sir Winston Churchill's house,' Harry's dad said, as he bit into the scone.

'I'll show you round the gardens once it stops snowing,' Old Ned said. 'Even in November they're full of wonderful smells. The thyme in the vegetable garden's been particularly abundant this year.'

'I learnt market gardening thanks to a charity for blind veterans called St Dunstan's,' Harry's dad told Ned. 'As well as poultry farming. But I preferred the gardening.'

'Chartwell's always prided itself on growing its own fruit and vegetables,' Ned said. 'The orchard's overflowing in the summer and we could always do with another man to help.'

'I'm sure you could,' Harry's dad said.

'So,' Ned said. 'What do you think?'

'About what?' Harry's dad asked him, looking confused.

'About coming to work here.'

'Me?'

'I don't see any other people with market gardening experience in the room.'

'But I'm blind.'

'And I'm old, doesn't stop me working,' Old Ned laughed.

Harry's dad laughed too, looking amazed and excited, but then paused:

'What about my guide dog? Mr Jenner has a dog that he wants to train for me. Her name's Callie.'

'I know she'll be perfect.' Mr Jenner said, with his mouth full of scone.

'Dogs are more than welcome,' Old Ned said.

'Oh yes, we love dogs here,' Grace told him. 'And a steady sort of dog, like a guide dog, will make a nice friend for my Buttons.'

Buttons heard his name and gave Grace's hand a lick.

'Might even show you how to behave,' she told the puppy as she gave him a stroke.

'I'd love to work here,' Harry's dad said. 'Thank you for asking me. Thank you very much indeed.'

Little Houdini stalked his way over to Buttons across the carpet. When he got to the puppy's face he put his paw out and gently tapped him on the nose. Buttons immediately dipped his head and front paws down with his bottom up and tail wagging in a play bow. Little Houdini sniffed at the puppy and Buttons wagged his tail even more. Soon the two young animals were playing again. This time wrestling and chasing each other as the others looked on and laughed.

Chapter 21

'It's like she was born to do this,' Mr Jenner told Harry, six months later, as they watched Callie and Harry's dad stop at a pavement kerb, listen for sounds and then cross together when it was safe to do so. He was thrilled that one more unwanted animal had found a home.

'She makes me feel like I've got my life back, like I can do anything and go anywhere,' Harry's dad said happily.

Old Ned had given them a dog basket as a present and from the first night Callie came home, both Little Houdini and the gentle Labrador shared it when they weren't sharing Harry's bed.

At Chartwell the scent of summer roses filled the air.

'That's it,' Old Ned said, and Harry stopped throwing the ball to look over at his dad and Old Ned transplanting basil seedlings together. His dad was smiling as he worked and that made Harry smile too. He still liked to help Mr Jenner at the RSPCA before and after school and he always proudly wore his Animal Defender badge, but he also spent lots of time at Chartwell with his dad on the weekends. They hadn't been able to do much together before, but now everything had changed.

Callie whined and Buttons put his paw on Harry's leg to remind him to throw the ball.

Harry threw it and the dogs ran down the path after it.

Callie got the ball first but she dropped it for Buttons to pick up and the poodle puppy brought it back to Harry, very proud of himself.

Little Houdini wasn't so little any more, but although he now looked like a cat he definitely still acted like a playful kitten. While Callie and Buttons played he sniffed at a sunflower, and tried to catch a bluebottle that buzzed past him, as well as a butterfly that landed on a pink-and-white hollyhock.

Little Houdini was such a determined cat and he still escaped every now and again, but he always came back after his little adventures.

'What's this?' Harry said excitedly, picking a flower. 'Look!'

Little Houdini was immediately interested and came running over to pounce on the long-stemmed dandelion that Harry wriggled along the path.

Callie and Buttons started to play-wrestle instead of bringing back the ball.

Little Houdini suddenly stopped stalking the weed stem and lifted his head as if he were listening to something in the distance. The next moment he ran off along the path and out of the vegetable garden.

'Where are you off to now?' Harry called after him. He hoped Little Houdini wasn't heading for the fish pond with the stepping stones across it where he'd found him swimming the day before. He didn't think Sir Winston Churchill would be pleased if the kitten caught one of his giant golden fishes. Not that Little Houdini could swim fast enough for that.

Harry sighed as he stood up. Little Houdini was living up to his name once again. He didn't know where the kitten was heading or why he seemed so intent as he ran. Mr Jenner said a cat's hearing was much more sensitive than people's, but Harry hadn't heard anything unusual.

Little Houdini ran across the orchard and miaowed outside a door, but no one came to open it. He hopped up on to the windowsill and miaowed again, louder this time.

'Little Houdini, come back!' Harry shouted, seeing the kitten outside the painting studio in the distance.

Little Houdini pushed at the window and slipped inside.

Peeping out from under the chair of a man sitting at an artist's easel was a marmalade kitten that looked almost exactly like Little Houdini. The two marmalade kittens stared at each other, their tails twitching.

'Well, who's this, Jock?' Sir Winston Churchill asked. 'Another kitty just like you. Will you be friends or foe I wonder?'

Harry didn't realize anyone was in the studio and so he burst in through the door without knocking only to find himself staring at the surprised face of Sir Winston Churchill.

'May I help you?' Sir Winston asked him.

Harry gulped. He certainly hadn't expected to meet Sir Winston Churchill for the first time like this. He felt his face going red.

'Yes. My name is Harry, and I'm . . . I'm following a marmalade kitten called Little Houdini,' he stammered.

He looked down at the floor and saw two marmalade kittens that could have been twins. Little Houdini and the other kitten purred and rubbed their faces together.

'Ah yes, these two seem to have become firm friends,' Sir Winston said, and Harry nodded.

The ex-prime minister used his walking stick to point at one of the kittens. 'That's Jock, a present for my eighty-eighth birthday last year. He's a rescue kitten. I presume the other is your Little Houdini?'

Harry opened his mouth but he was feeling so over-awed that no words came out. He crouched down, held out his hands and Jock came over to sniff his fingers. Meanwhile Little Houdini hopped up on to Sir Winston's lap and sniffed at the oil paint he'd been using to paint a picture.

Harry finally found his voice as he stroked Jock's soft marmalade fur.

'Little Houdini's a rescue kitten too. We think he's a feral kitten and he was very nearly your birthday present as well,' he said. Stroking the kitten was very soothing. He was glad that he hadn't had to let Little Houdini go.

'Really? Well it looks as if he found the right home after all,' Winston said with a twinkle in his eye.

Little Houdini wriggled out of Sir Winston's lap.

'He's very good at escaping though.'

Sir Winston chuckled. 'What a performer Houdini was and quite the escape artist!'

The two kittens chased after a feather that had blown in when Harry had opened the door.

'They'd make a beautiful painting,' Sir Winston said, as he watched them playing together.

'I saw a painting of your marmalade cat, Tango,' Harry said, 'when Little Houdini got lost and me and Miss Hamblin were trying to catch him.'

'Tango was always eating at the table and sleeping on my bed,' Sir Winston told Harry.

'Sometimes there was barely room for me too! But that's cats for you. During the war I had a grey cat called Nelson, who I first met when I was at the Admiralty, and I even named after the famous Admiral Nelson. Let me tell you how I first met him.'

Chapter 22

The thin grey cat stalked the rat down the central London street, intent on his prey. He was just about to pounce on it when the rat scurried up some steps and disappeared in through the open door of a building. The hungry cat yeowled in despair and leapt up the steps after it. At the very same moment, a huge grizzled stray dog spotted the cat and went racing into the building after him. The cat was gaining on the rat when it squeezed through the metal bars of the grate of an unlit fireplace.

The cat was too big to get through the grate, but it crouched down and pushed its paw through the gap, intent on its prey.

Behind the cat, in the passageway of the building, the dog growled and showed its sharp teeth. The cat's hackles rose and it spun round, arched its back and ran at the dog. This wasn't the first time the cat had had to defend himself.

When the dog saw that the cat wasn't afraid of him he gave a yelp of terror and raced back out of the front door with his tail between his legs.

'What a brave cat,' said a round man wearing a trilby hat, who was standing on the steps. 'Well done, cat, for protecting the Admiralty!'

To the grey cat's great surprise, he was picked up by the man. He considered jumping out of the round man's arms, but he was tired and it was a comfortable spot.

'Anyone know where he comes from?' the man asked.

No one had ever seen the cat before and judging by how thin he was and the poor condition of his coat, they all agreed that he was probably a stray.

'He seems quite taken with you, Prime Minister,' his secretary said, smiling.

'You're coming home with me and I shall call you Nelson,' Mr Churchill said, and he gave the grey cat to his secretary to hold on the short journey from the Admiralty to 10 Downing Street, glancing at Admiral Nelson's tall column in Trafalgar Square as he got into the car.

'Salmon for my new cat friend Nelson,' Mr Churchill commanded as he arrived at Number 10. 'The bravest cat in all of England.'

'Yes, Prime Minister,' said the butler and he hurried off to open a tin.

Nelson was very hungry and gulped down the salmon and another tin on top of that! When he'd finished, he licked his lips and looked up at Mr Churchill.

'Nothing like a good meal to set you up for the day,' the prime minister told the cat, patting his own tummy.

Nelson followed him to his room and hopped up on to Mr Churchill's bed beside him and purred.

'You have a nice sleep while I get on with my war work,' the prime minister said, giving Nelson a stroke. With his belly full and a soft bed to lie on Nelson soon did just that.

When he woke up there was a small brown poodle on the floor by the bed. Nelson hissed at it but the dog only wagged its tail and looked at the man who had papers in his hands.

'There, there, Nelson. Don't be a brute,' Winston Churchill told the cat. 'There's room enough for both of you.'

The little dog kept on wagging its tail and after Nelson had had a good sniff of him he let the dog jump up on to the bed with him.

'Good cat, Nelson,' Mr Churchill said, putting down his papers to stroke both animals. 'And good dog too, Rufus!'

'Toby, Toby, my name is Toby,' chirped a voice and Nelson looked up to see a blue budgerigar in a round cage.

Nelson licked his lips, stalked across the bed over to the cage and stared up at the bird.

'Toby, Toby, my name is Toby,' the budgerigar chirped again.

Nelson gave a miaow and looked back at Winston Churchill.

'Oh no, he's not for eating, my dear,' Winston said. 'And I'll be very displeased if you try to do so.'

Nelson came back to Winston and Rufus, rolled over on his back purring happily and waiting for his tummy to be stroked by the prime minister's pudgy fingers.

'That's a good cat.'

It didn't take long for Nelson to stop being so skinny. When Mrs Churchill wasn't looking the prime minister sneaked pieces of chicken from his plate to the cat at dinner time and there was always plenty of tinned salmon. He was so full up that Nelson wasn't the least bit tempted to try to catch Toby when the budgerigar was let out of the cage and flew around the room.

The once hungry and homeless cat had found the perfect home.

Chapter 23

Sir Winston smiled down at Little Houdini and Jock playing together.

'Nelson was lucky that he met you,' Harry said shyly. 'And found a good home. We get lots of animals needing new homes at the RSPCA.'

Sir Winston nodded. 'There have been so many cats, and other animals, over the years and all of them unique and much loved in their own way,' he said.

Jock hopped up on to Sir Winston's lap and Little Houdini followed his friend, but decided to sit in the spot where Sir Winston's neck met his shoulder.

Harry put his hand over his mouth to hide a smile. Little Houdini was always doing that to people he liked.

'Time for some fresh air, Harry,' Sir Winston said, tapping at the wheelchair beside him with his walking stick. 'I've always said that a day spent away from Chartwell is a day wasted, and my chariot awaits. If you wouldn't mind giving me a push?'

Harry was more than happy to do so and ran over to help Sir Winston into his wheelchair.

'Good lad,' Sir Winston said as he sat down, and they headed out of the painting studio with Little Houdini and Jock scampering along behind them.

'My dad won't believe I've met you,' Harry blurted.

'Where is your dad?' Sir Winston asked him.

'He's working in the vegetable garden with Ned.' Harry said proudly.

'Well, let's go there then,' Sir Winston said, showing the way by pointing his walking stick as if it were a lance and his wheelchair a horse.

Harry grinned as he pushed Sir Winston down the path. He knew his dad would be over the moon to meet Sir Winston.

As they approached the red-brick wall with an arch in it that led to the vegetable garden Sir Winston said: 'I built that wall. Used to be a dab hand at bricklaying once upon a time.'

The two kittens ran along beside the chair stalking a mouse before being distracted by a cabbage white butterfly.

'I hope Jock's not frightened of guide dogs,' Harry said. 'My dad's guide dog Callie would never hurt him and Little Houdini loves him, but sometimes cats don't know that.'

'Jock won't be scared,' Sir Winston said. 'He's a brave cat, although not as brave as Nelson was. Wars and bombs are terrifying for animals and people too. I hope we never have another like the last.'

The cabbage white butterfly flew away but a red admiral one took its place and the two kittens chased after that instead.

Harry saw that his dad and Old Ned were just ahead. They had their heads close together as they worked. Callie was snoozing close by in the warm afternoon sun.

'Well, hello there!' Sir Winston called out, waving his walking stick in the air.

'Sir,' Harry's dad said, recognizing Sir Winston's distinctive voice even if he couldn't see him. He immediately stood to attention and almost dropped the plant pot he was holding. Fortunately Old Ned was there to catch it.

'At ease, soldier,' said Sir Winston. 'No need for formality here. Hello, Ned, my old friend.'

'Winny,' Old Ned said, as the two of them patted each other on the back in a friendly hug. Callie woke up and came running over, tail wagging, wanting to join in too.

'Who's this then?' Sir Winston asked, stroking the yellow Labrador. 'What a lovely dog.'

'That's Callie,' Harry said.

'Sorry, sir,' said Harry's dad. 'She likes to say hello to everyone.'

'Don't apologize,' Sir Winston told him. 'The more pets the merrier, I say. And dogs are a man's best friend after all.'

Jock gave a miaow and Sir Winston chuckled.

'Oh, all right,' he said, as if he understood exactly what Jock was trying to say. 'Cats are wonderful too.'

Jock miaowed again and Sir Winston added, 'Even more wonderful perhaps. Cats have been loyal companions and friends and foot-warmers to me my whole life. Remember Sergeant Tommy, Ned?'

Ned nodded. 'I'll never forget him. He was the first of many marmalade cats over the years.'

The red admiral butterfly had flown over the wall and Jock and Little Houdini were now lying in a sunny spot over by the sunflowers.

'I'm so glad dear Jock has a cat friend to play with at Chartwell,' Sir Winston said.

Little Houdini stretched out his paws and rolled over on to his back and Jock did the same.

'They look so happy together,' said Harry.

He'd never forget the day he'd rescued the muddy little feral kitten and everything that had happened since.

Sir Winston smiled and nodded. 'They do. You know, I think there should always be a marmalade rescue cat living at Chartwell; napping in sunny spots, chasing butterflies through the long grass and eating until their tummy's full.'

Everyone agreed that would be perfect.

And so there was.

Acknowledgements

The story of how Sir Winston Churchill wished there always to be a cat like his own beloved marmalade one, Jock, living at his home in Chartwell, Kent, helped to inspire this book. Sir Winston loved animals and had pets throughout his life, including two miniature brown poodles, both called Rufus. He also gave a miniature black poodle to Grace Hamblin, his secretary for over 30 years, who became the first curator of Chartwell after Sir Winston died. Along with Jock the cat, Grace's poodle

met some of the early visitors to the house –
and one of them wrote about meeting not one
but two marmalade cats.

It was a bitterly cold day in Kent when I met
my brother, Robin, his partner, Eunice, and my
niece, Jasmine, at the estate. We didn't get to
meet the current resident cat (Jock number six),
but I loved hearing tales of Jasmine's own
marmalade cat, Amber. I took one of my
golden retrievers, Freya, with me and she was
made very welcome by the Chartwell staff, and
enjoyed all the strokes and fusses that were
made of her as well as a tasty snack from the
cafe. Freya had only just finished eating it when
snow began to fall. In no time at all, we were
surrounded by swirling snow and grit was being
laid so cars could drive out of the car park. All
in all, our visit was an unforgettable experience.

Researching and writing this book has been
an absolute delight and I would like to thank

my amazing editor Carmen McCullough, copy-editors Bea McIntyre and Frances Evans, and proofreaders Mary Finch and Sally Boyles. The cover for *Winston and the Marmalade Cat* is beautiful, thanks to the talents of artist Angelo Rinaldi and designer Jan Bielecki. On the PR and marketing side huge thanks must go to Jasmine Joynson and Lucie Sharpe, along with sales experts Tineke Mollemans and Kirsty Bradbury. My agent and friend Clare Pearson of Eddison Pearson has been with me throughout most of my career and made it a much happier one than it would have been without her ☺

Lastly to my dogs Bella and Freya who inspire me every day and are currently waiting to go to the river for a walk. As well, as always, to my dear husband, Eric.

Quiz Time!

How well do you know the story of *Winston and the Marmalade Cat?*

Questions:

1. Which animal did Sir Winston get as a birthday present?
2. Where did Harry rescue the kitten from?
3. What did Mr Jenner feed the rescued kitten at the RSPCA centre?
4. What was the name of Sir Winston Churchill's home in Kent?

5. What was Harry's teacher's name?

6. When was VE day?

7. Why did Harry call the cat Little Houdini?

8. Why doesn't Harry like Sir Winston Churchill at the beginning of the story?

9. What badge was Harry given for rescuing the kitten?

10. What nickname did Ned give to Winston Churchill when they were children?

11. What did Winston's school report say about him?

12. How much stronger is a cat's sense of smell than a human's?

13. What job is Harry's dad given at Chartwell?

14. What was the name of Harry's dad's guide dog?

15. Who was Churchill's grey homeless cat named after?

Answers:

1. A marmalade cat
2. A pipe
3. Goat's milk with an egg yolk and a little sugar
4. Chartwell
5. Mrs Dunbar
6. 8 May 1945
7. He had escaped his cage three times, as if by magic!
8. Harry blamed Churchill for his dad's blindness
9. An Animal Defenders badge
10. Winny
11. That he would never amount to much
12. It's fourteen times stronger than a human's
13. Gardener
14. Callie
15. Admiral Nelson

Scrumptious Scones

Harry, Old Ned and Grace love tea and scones, especially after they've been running around after Little Houdini in the snow. Have a go at making your own delicious scones using this recipe!

The recipe makes enough for eight people, so you can share with your friends and family too.

Remember to ask an adult to help you, as you'll be using a hot oven (and making a mess in the kitchen!).

You will need:

- 350g self-raising flour
- Pinch of salt
- 1 tsp baking powder
- 85g butter (cut this into cubes)
- 3 tbsp caster sugar
- 175ml milk
- 1 egg, beaten (for glazing)
- A mixing bowl
- A jug
- A biscuit cutter
- A baking tray

How to make them:

1. Heat your oven to 220°C/Gas mark 7.
2. Tip the flour into a large bowl with the salt and baking powder, then mix.

3. Rub the butter into the flour mix with your fingers until the mix looks like small, even crumbs.

4. Stir in the sugar.

5. Put the milk into a microwavable jug or bowl, and heat for about 30 seconds until warm.

6. Make a well in the flour mix using your fingers, then add the milk and combine slowly. Don't worry if it seems a bit wet at first; you will end up with a soft dough that does not feel sticky.

7. At this point, you will need to ask an adult to put a baking tray in the oven to warm up for use later.

8. Scatter some extra flour on to the work top and tip the dough out.

9. Dust the dough with a little more flour, then fold it over 2–3 times so it becomes a little smoother.

10. Here comes the fun bit! Pat your dough gently out until it is about 4-cm thick.

11. Make sure an adult is nearby to help, then push the cutter into the dough with all your muscles! Repeat until you have used up all the dough. You can roll the leftover bits of dough into one and pat back out for cutting.

12. Brush the tops of the scones with the beaten egg. Now ask an adult to help you place them on to the hot baking tray.

13. Bake for 10 minutes until they have risen and turned a yummy golden colour on top. Remove from the oven and set them on a baking rack.

14. And finally . . . the best bit! Eat the scones warm or cold on the day you baked them. Harry recommends eating scones with cream and lashings of strawberry jam. Or why not try some marmalade, for a Little Houdini twist?

The Life of Sir Winston Churchill

Now find out a bit more about the life of Sir Winston Churchill!

About

Winston Churchill was Britain's famous wartime leader. He was the Prime Minister of Great Britain during the Second World War.

He was born at Blenheim Palace, near Oxford, in 1874.

He was best known for his resilience against Hitler and the Nazis, as well as his rousing speeches.

He died in 1965, having lived through both the First and Second World Wars.

Early Life

Poor Winston never really enjoyed school and he was not very highly regarded by his teachers either. He often got into trouble and his school report famously said that he 'would never amount to much'. How wrong they were!

It has been said that Churchill struggled with a lisp as a child, but that didn't stop him from becoming one of the most famous and inspiring public speakers in British history.

War and Adventures

Churchill never shied away from adventure, and after leaving school he travelled to many exotic faraway places, working as reporter in America and Cuba, and fighting in the army in the Boer War.

After working as an MP, he became Prime Minister in May 1940, leading Britain in the war against the Nazis. He was well liked and boosted the morale of British citizens by walking through London during the Blitz and making the 'V' sign for victory.

Pet Lover

Churchill loved animals, and had many wonderful pets through the years. Many of which you will recognize from this story: Rufus the poodle and Rufus 2; his cats, Nelson and Jock; as well as pigs, a bulldog, goldfish, black swans, butterflies, kangaroos and even a lion!

If you've enjoyed the story of Winston and his marmalade cat, you'll love reading about King Charles II's spaniel Tiger Lily and her friend Woofer in *The Great Fire Dogs*.

Turn the page for a little taste.

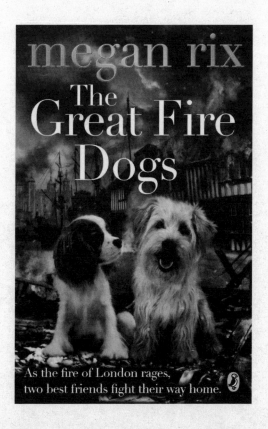

Chapter 1

February 1666

On the snow-covered south side of the River
Thames, a red-faced man wearing a patched,
woollen green coat and a grubby, rust-coloured
waistcoat stood next to a wicker basket.
Squashed inside the basket were six dock-tailed
Wicklow terrier puppies.

'Wheelers – wheeler pups for sale!' the man
shouted into the icy-cold air. He blew on his
fingers to try and warm them up. Next to him,

a man was roasting chestnuts on a fire but the dog seller couldn't afford to buy any until he'd sold a puppy. He pulled the lid off the wicker basket beside him, reached into it and grabbed the first puppy he touched by the scruff of its neck. 'These little dogs were born to work in the kitchen,' he called out to the passing people as the cream-coated puppy tried to wriggle free. 'Born to turn the cooking wheel.'

In the wicker basket, one of the puppies, the one who had been getting squashed by the first puppy's bottom, popped his head out to look at the snowy winter scene. The snow had come down hard overnight and London had woken covered in a thick white coat. There were stalls positioned all along the white banks of the river, many of them selling food. Hot pies and roast meat as well as chestnuts and gingerbread. The puppy sniffed at the delicious smells in the air and gave a whine.

'My turnspit dog got out during the plague

last year and that was the last I saw of him,' a woman with an apron over her long brown skirt told the puppy seller. 'Caught by one of those awful dog catchers, no doubt.'

The puppy seller nodded. There used to be lots of dogs and cats in London's streets, most of them strays, but not any more. They were thought to carry the plague and people had been paid good money to catch and kill them.

The king's official order had been that: '*No Swine, Dogs, Cats or tame Pigeons be permitted to pass up and down in Streets, or from house to house, in places Infected.*' But the lord mayor of London had taken things a step further and ordered all stray cats and dogs to be put down, just like the last time there'd been a plague and the time before that too.

'I heard forty thousand dogs and two hundred thousand cats lost their lives,' the dog seller told the woman.

While they were talking, the puppy that had

been looking out of the top of the basket scrambled free and headed off on his short puppy legs towards the frozen water's edge.

On the other side of the river, across the long bridge full of houses and shops, twelve-year-old George, palace kitchen apprentice, looked over at the skaters on the wide expanse of frozen water. Their sharp, iron-bladed skates made swishing sounds as they cut through the ice like butter. He watched in admiration as they weaved in and out of the arches under London Bridge. The bridge acted like a weir, turning the water sluggish so it was more likely to freeze. In places the ice was more than five feet thick and perfect for skating. George wished he could skate.

Some winters, when the vast Thames froze even harder than this, they held Frost Fairs on the river. Stalls were set up on the ice and people walked about on the river as if it were a street, but it wasn't frozen enough for that yet.

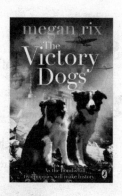
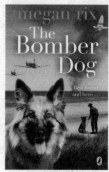
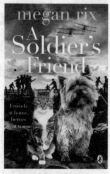

A PUFFIN BOOK

stories that last a lifetime

Ever wanted a friend who could take you to magical realms, talk to animals or help you survive a shipwreck? Well, you'll find them all in the **A PUFFIN BOOK** collection.

A PUFFIN BOOK will stay with you **forever**. Maybe you'll read it again and again, or perhaps years from now you'll suddenly **remember** the moment it made you **laugh** or **cry** or simply see things **differently**. Adventurers **big** and **small**, rebels out to **change** their world, even a mouse with a **dream** and a spider who can spell – these are the characters who make **stories** that last a **lifetime**.

Whether you love animal tales, war stories or want to know what it was like growing up in a different time and place, the **A PUFFIN BOOK** collection has a story for you – you just need to decide where you want to go next . . .